Don't Tell Anyone

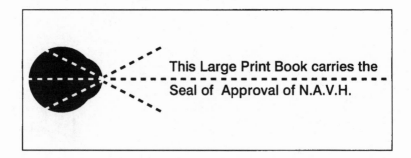

This Large Print Book carries the
Seal of Approval of N.A.V.H.

Don't Tell Anyone

PEG KEHRET

Thorndike Press • Waterville, Maine

Published in 2002 by arrangement with Dutton Children's Books, a member of Penguin Putnam, Inc.

Thorndike Press Large Print Juvenile Series.

The tree indicium is a trademark of Thorndike Press.

The text of this Large Print edition is unabridged.
Other aspects of the book may vary from the original edition.

Set in 16 pt. Plantin by Christina S. Huff.

Printed in the United States on permanent paper.

Library of Congress Cataloging-in-Publication Data

Kehret, Peg.
    Don't tell anyone / Peg Kehret.
      p. cm.
    Summary: Twelve-year-old Megan does not realize that feeding a group of feral cats living in a field near her house will involve her as a witness to a traffic accident and in the dangerous plan of an unstable criminal.
    ISBN 0-7862-4516-6 (lg. print : hc : alk. paper)
    1. Large type books. [1. Feral cats — Fiction. 2. Cats — Fiction. 3. Single-parent families — fiction. 4. Criminals — Fiction. 5. Large type books.] I. Title.
PZ7.K2518 Dq 2002
  [Fic]—dc21   2002028545

For my grandsons,
Eric Carl Konen and Mark Edward Kehret,
with love from Moonie

1

Megan discovered the cats by accident. She was roller-skating on the sidewalk beside the field when one of her wheels came off. As it sailed into the tall weeds, a black-and-white cat flew out, streaked across the sidewalk, and disappeared into a large drainpipe.

Megan landed on her hands and knees. Unhurt, she crawled into the weeds and found the wheel. The nut that had come loose still lay on the sidewalk, so Megan re-attached the wheel, tightening the nut with her fingers. She hoped it would hold until she got home and could use a wrench.

She knelt by the drainpipe and peered inside. Two amber eyes stared back.

"Hello, kitty," Megan said.

"Hiss!"

"Nice pussycat," Megan said. "I won't hurt you."

The cat hissed again and backed farther into the drainpipe.

"Here, kitty, kitty. Nice, kitty." Megan

wondered if the cat was a lost pet. Maybe the cat had a collar with an identification tag. If so, Megan would call the owner and say she'd found the cat.

Slowly Megan put her hand inside the drainpipe.

Slash! The cat's claws ripped across the top of Megan's hand. She jerked her arm back and put her hand to her mouth.

I knew better than to stick my hand in there, she thought, as she pressed her hand to her jeans to stop the bleeding.

She sat on the sidewalk to wait. If she was quiet, the cat would think she had left, and it might come out. Then she could see if there was a collar or not. If the cat wouldn't let her touch it, she would get a good description so she could look in the lost-and-found ads to see if anyone was missing a cat like this one.

While she waited, Megan watched cars go up the freeway on-ramp. She also saw movement in the grassy field. Soon a large orange cat leaped forward, pouncing on something in the weeds. When he raised his head a moment later, a field mouse dangled from his teeth.

Megan wondered how many cats lived in this field. She sat quietly, watching both the weeds and the drainpipe.

The cat never emerged from the drainpipe, but in the hour that Megan waited she glimpsed two more cats in the field. Both of them fled when she called, "Here, kitty, kitty."

She wondered how the cats had gotten there. Had someone dumped a box of unwanted kittens and they had managed to survive?

Megan went home to get her shoes and money, then went to the mini-mart to buy a bag of cat food. Back home again, she took a pie plate from the kitchen cupboard, filled it with cat food, and carried it the four blocks from her house to the field.

She saw no cats. Kneeling, she peered into the drainpipe. It was empty.

A lone maple tree grew in the center of the field. Megan put the plate of food in the grass at the base of the tree. Then she climbed the tree and sat on a limb to wait.

About fifteen minutes later, a scrawny black-and-white cat approached the pie plate. Megan wondered if this was the cat that had scratched her.

The cat slunk forward cautiously, his belly only an inch above the ground. He ate a few bites, stopped and looked around, then ate some more. Soon he was joined by an orange cat that had a nick out of one ear. Megan thought that it was the cat she had seen catch a mouse. Next a scruffy gray cat arrived.

Megan expected the cats to fight over the food, with the first ones keeping the late arrivals away, but that didn't happen. Instead, as each cat approached, the others looked up briefly and then continued to eat. Soon the pie plate looked like the center of a wheel, with multicolored cats angling out like spokes all the way around it.

Hidden by maple leaves, Megan sat still and watched. She decided to name each of the cats. The black-and-white one was Claws, because of the scratch on Megan's hand. The orange one was Pumpkin, and the gray one became Twitchy Tail.

One of the cats, a brown-and-tan striped tabby, was much plumper than the rest. Suspecting that the cat was pregnant, Megan named her Mommacat.

When the food was gone, the cats scattered — all except Mommacat, who licked the bottom of the empty dish and then sat washing her whiskers. She's still hungry, Megan thought. I need to bring more food next time.

She decided to bring cat food to the field every day. When Mommacat's kittens were born, Megan would make sure they were all right. Maybe when they were old enough, she could take one home and keep it. Megan and Kylie, her little sister, had begged for years to get a pet, but Mom said animals took too much time.

"We'll get one when you're older," Mom always said, "and more responsible. We'll talk about it when you're older." Megan had turned twelve last month; maybe she was finally old enough.

Megan shifted position; Mommacat looked up in alarm, then bolted away. Megan climbed down, picked up the pie plate, and headed for home.

The next day she brought more food, plus an old soup bowl and a peanut-butter jar full of water. She poured the water into the bowl and put it beside the food. When the cats came, they lapped the water eagerly. Megan realized mice were probably plentiful in the field, but water might be scarce. After that, she brought food and fresh water every day.

When she returned home on the third day of feeding the cats, Megan's mother was in the kitchen, pouring a cup of coffee.

"Chelsea called," Mrs. Perk said. "She wants you to call her."

Megan's best friend, Chelsea, lived just two blocks away. The girls often played together after school. This week, however, Chelsea had chicken pox.

Megan washed the pie plate.

"Don't try to pet those cats when you feed them," Mrs. Perk warned. "Feral cats are wild things. They'll scratch and bite. Probably none of them has been vaccinated for rabies. A scratch from a wild cat can be serious."

Megan looked down at the slash on the back of her hand. It was puffed and angry looking, much redder than it had been the day it happened.

Mrs. Perk's eyes followed Megan's glance. "What's that? Have you already been scratched?"

Megan nodded.

"Let me see your hand," Mom said.

Reluctantly, Megan extended her hand toward her mother.

"Did you put antiseptic on it?"

"No. It looked okay until today."

"It doesn't look okay now. I'll get the first-aid kit."

After swabbing the wound with antiseptic, Mrs. Perk said, "You had better stay away from that field. We'll be lucky if you don't end up with an infection."

"But the cats need me," Megan said. "You should see how glad they are to get fresh water, and they eat every crumb of food."

"They got along before you found them."

"One of them is pregnant. She looks as if her kittens will arrive at any second."

"They aren't your cats," Mrs. Perk said.

"But what if the mother cat needs help? What if there's a problem when the kittens are born?"

"Wild animals know how to take care of themselves, and those cats are definitely wild animals."

"I'll be careful," Megan promised. "Since that first day, all I do is set the food and water down, and then I climb a tree and watch the cats eat. I don't try to touch them."

The phone in Mrs. Perk's office rang. She hurried to answer it. Megan's mother worked for a stock brokerage firm. She had her home computer networked to the office and did much of her work from home.

Her reason for working this way was that, as a divorced mother, she wanted to be at home to supervise her daughters. In truth, however, even though Mrs. Perk was there physically, she rarely had time during the week to pay close attention to what Megan or Kylie were doing. Megan often wished she and Mom could finish a conversation without being interrupted by one of Mom's clients.

Because of the time difference between

the West Coast, where the Perks lived, and New York, where the Stock Exchange is located, Mrs. Perk was on the telephone by six-thirty every morning. Megan usually fixed breakfast for herself and Kylie, made sure Kylie got on the kindergarten bus, and then rode her bike to school.

After school Mrs. Perk took calls from clients, worked on their portfolios, and researched companies to determine if their stock was likely to go up in value. She supervised Kylie's after-school play, but Megan was allowed to come and go, as long as she left a note or told her mother where she was.

Weekends were better. On Saturday afternoons, Mrs. Perk took her daughters hiking or swimming or bowling. Sometimes Megan and Kylie each got to invite a friend to go along.

Megan waited a long time for her mother to get off the phone. While she waited, she remembered her mother's instructions. "Maybe you had better stay away from that field." Her mother had not told her she had to stay away. She had said *maybe*.

The cats did need the food and water, especially Mommacat, whose sides now pushed out so far she looked like a bubble that was ready to burst. The phone conversation went on; Megan gave up waiting.

The next morning Megan wanted to stay home from school and go to the field to wait for the kittens to be born. But she knew what her mother would say to that request, so she didn't bother to ask.

Instead she carried the cat food and her jar of water to school in her backpack. After school, Megan rushed for her bike, removed the padlock, and pedaled as fast as she could toward the field.

She hoped she wasn't too late. She wanted to be there when the kittens were born.

About a block before she got to the field, something white caught her attention. Oh no, Megan thought, as she saw that a large white sign had been erected on the edge of the field. Filled with anxiety, she rode toward it.

Megan had seen such signs before. They went up on vacant lots as a way to announce to the neighborhood that the lot would not be vacant for long.

The woods where Megan and Kylie used to play had been cut down last year, soon after such a sign was erected. Dozens of new houses now stood where the woods used to be, and the first thing each of the new owners did after they moved in was plant some trees.

She stopped her bike next to the sign.

FUTURE HOME OF
EVERGREEN APARTMENTS.
160 LUXURY UNITS.

Megan's heart sank. Someone was going to build apartments on this field. But what about the cats? Megan wondered. What will happen to them?

She remembered the enormous rumbling bulldozers that had flattened the woods in such a brief time. She imagined the panic of the cats as they ran to escape the huge, noisy machines. Where would they go? Onto the freeway?

I have to help them, Megan thought. I have to find a way to catch the cats and tame them and find homes for them before the field gets leveled.

I have to keep the apartment complex from being built until the cats are safe.

But how?

2

Tuesday night, Shane Turner unlocked the office of Colby Construction Company, stepped inside, and locked the door behind him. He did not switch on any lights; there was no point calling attention to the fact that the building was occupied so late at night. What if Brice Colby, Shane's brother-in-law, happened to drive past? If Brice saw a light, he'd be in there in a flash, asking Shane what he was doing, and then what would Shane say?

Brice did not know that Shane had a key to the office. It had been easy to get; Shane simply pretended to have trouble with his truck one morning. He borrowed his sister's car for the day, then made duplicate keys of everything on Ruthann Colby's key ring before he returned the car.

The office windows faced the parking lot. Shane looked out. His blue pickup was the only vehicle parked there.

Colorful hammers and wrenches floated

on the computer's screen-saver program. Shane walked to the glowing screen.

He uncovered the keyboard, then punched in the commands for Colby Construction's bookkeeping program. The first time he had done this, two weeks earlier, it had taken him three tries to correctly guess the password. He had tried Brice's birthday first, and then Ruthann's birthday. When those didn't work, he tried their wedding anniversary, November 23, and the Colby accounts appeared on the screen.

When the system asked for the password this time, Shane typed in 1123. Next he clicked on *Accounts Payable.*

While he waited for the information to appear, he wiped his sweaty hands on his jeans. The blue screen gave an eerie glow to that corner of the dark office.

Shane typed in *Bradburn Cement Company,* a nonexistent business. He typed *Amount due for work completed on Bayview Place,* a furniture store that Colby Construction was presently building.

He made the check payable to William Bradburn. One of Shane's driver's licenses was in that name; he would use it for identification when he cashed the check.

Shane could type in the amount of money that Colby Construction "owed" William

Bradburn and print out a check, and no one would know. He had done it once before, and neither Brice nor the bookkeeper had caught on.

Although Shane knew he was alone, his heart raced as he typed the numbers: $15,104.23. He made the amount uneven so that it would look more like a real billing from the fictitious cement company.

Shane pressed *Print Check*. The machine that printed checks warmed up; the pale green paper slid forward, and the finished check emerged from the other side.

Shane held it toward the glow from the computer screen, making sure that it was made out properly. If the check didn't match Shane's fake driver's license, he'd never be able to cash it.

The check was perfect. Shane forged Brice's signature on the bottom of the check. He had practiced it so many times, he could do it without even looking at Brice's real signature.

Shane put the check in his wallet, then exited the bookkeeping program. The dancing hammers and wrenches returned to the screen.

A band of light flashed across the wall as a car drove into the parking lot. Shane's heart pounded. He hurried to the window and looked out, keeping to the side of the glass where he could not be seen. He did not recognize the car.

The car made a U-turn, went out the same driveway it had come in, and drove off.

This is the last time I'll do this, Shane promised himself. It was too risky. If Brice ever found out, Shane knew he would lose not only his job, but his freedom.

When Shane had been released from prison six months earlier, his sister, Ruthann, had pleaded with Brice to give her brother a job. No one else was willing to take a chance on an ex-con with a record of armed robbery and forgery.

Brice had not wanted to take a chance, either. He made it clear when he hired Shane that Shane was on trial and that if he made one wrong move, he would never work for Colby Construction again. Brice also made it clear that he would prosecute any illegal activity.

"You're here because you're my wife's brother," Brice had said on the first day of Shane's employment. "You've lied to her for years and gotten away with it, but lies won't work with me. If you do the job right, keep your temper under control, and stay out of trouble, you can work for me as long as you want to. But there won't be any second chance if you slip up. Is that clear?"

It was clear, all right. It was clear to Shane that Brice would always be the boss, that Brice would always make more money than Shane did, and that Brice thought he was doing Shane a huge favor.

Well, Shane didn't want any more favors. He was sick of pounding nails in unheated buildings. He was tired of getting his boots muddy and of having his back ache at the end of the day. He was ready to move on, but he knew he couldn't just up and leave. He needed a plan, and he needed money.

He'd had the plan for almost a month, ever since Brice had reluctantly agreed to let Shane pilot the hot-air balloon that Colby Construction was sponsoring in the town's annual balloon festival.

Now Shane had the money to carry out his plan.

Brice had never found out about the first forged check, for seven hundred dollars, that Shane had printed and cashed. He would never know about this one, either. Even if the bookkeeper discovered the fictitious Bradburn account, it would take awhile before anyone suspected Shane.

Brice and Ruthann didn't even know that Shane could use the computer. Shane had learned how in prison, as part of a training program that was supposed to prepare him to get a job. But he had kept that skill to himself. When Ruthann talked about all the information she found on the Internet, Shane pretended ignorance, as if using a computer was completely beyond his ability.

He had spent the stolen seven hundred dollars to buy an old clunker car, which he registered under the name William Bradburn. The car was already parked at Shane's getaway spot, the remote meadow on the other side of Desolation Hill, where Shane planned to land the Colby Construction hot-air balloon and set it afire to make it look as if he had crashed.

Ruthann would be devastated to think Shane had died in the crash; Brice would probably be relieved to be rid of him.

Shane was positive he would not get caught. He would not be charged with theft, and he would never, ever, return to prison. The eighteen months he had spent behind bars were the worst months of his life. He did not intend to repeat them.

Friday night, Shane would be out of this town. He had better things to do with his life than accept favors from his brother-in-law.

Shane knew that as long as all the Colby Construction projects moved forward as scheduled, there was little chance that the missing funds would be noticed. Brice's business was booming, which meant that large amounts of money flowed into the account, and large amounts were paid out for supplies and labor.

Colby Construction had an office building nearly completed, and Shane knew the company would break ground next week on a big apartment complex. That alone would put so much money into the account that a mere fifteen thousand would never be missed.

The only thing that could mess up Shane's plan would be if Brice's next job got delayed, so that the big money did not arrive as expected. If that happened, a shortage in the account might be discovered.

Nothing was going to delay the apartment complex. No neighbors would complain about a building that was erected right next to a freeway on-ramp. The apartment would not cause an environmental problem, and the impact on traffic would not matter in that location.

The building permit was expected on Thursday, and Brice was ready to start construction. Shane had arranged to have the field cleared on Friday, to make sure the project was under way before he left. By

Friday night, Shane would be gone.

Shane slipped outside, locked the office door behind him, and headed for his truck. The night air was warm; summer was almost here. Perfect weather to build an apartment complex, Shane thought. Nothing, not even rainy weather, would hold up Brice's big project — and nothing would keep Shane from using his cash to get out of this crummy town.

Shane knew exactly where he would go: New Mexico. There was a hot-air balloon festival in Albuquerque every year, and Shane planned to fly his own balloon in the next one.

Before he was sent to prison, Shane had gotten a license to be a hot-air balloon pilot. He had taken the required ten hours of instruction, passed a written and a verbal test, and then passed the flight exam. The license had cost him nearly fifteen hundred dollars, but it had been worth it.

Ever since he got his pilot's license he had wanted his own balloon business. Now *there* was a job worth having! The trouble was, it took money to buy the balloon and the basket. Even used balloons cost several thousand dollars.

Balloon owners need a place to keep their equipment, and they have to purchase propane, pay a ground crew, and advertise for customers. That's why he had robbed the bank three years ago; he had been trying to get cash to buy a hot-air balloon.

Shane finally had enough money, right there in his wallet. All he had to do was cash the check. In two days it would be Good-bye, Colby Construction. Good-bye, brother-in-law boss. Hello, independence.

Shane got in his pickup and drove out of the parking lot. On his way home, he passed the field where the apartment complex would be built. He saw that Brice had put up a sign, announcing his plans.

Sometimes such signs created a flurry of protest from neighbors, but he was certain this one wouldn't.

Who would object to an apartment building here?

3

Twitchy Tail was the first to come for food the day Megan saw the sign. He was soon followed by Pumpkin. A bedraggled white cat, its long fur full of matts, also slunk out of the weeds. Megan hadn't seen that one before. She named it Slush, because it was the dirty color of melting snowbanks in the spring.

While she watched them, Megan fretted about the apartment building. Finally Mommacat, her sides still bulging, arrived to eat. When the cats finished eating, Megan rushed home, eager to talk to Mom and ask what she thought Megan should do.

The door to her mother's office was closed, the signal that Megan and Kylie were not to bother her unless it was a matter of life or death. It is, Megan thought grimly, but she didn't knock. She knew life or death for the cats was not what Mom meant.

She heard her mother's voice from the other side of the door, quoting some statistics.

Megan decided to see if Kylie knew how long Mom would be busy.

Kylie was in her bedroom. As usual, she was singing. No matter what Kylie did, she sang about it while she did it. What's worse, all the songs had the same tune: "Row, Row, Row Your Boat." She made up the words as she went along.

Listening to Kylie made Megan want to cover her ears and run the other way, but she headed for her sister's room.

Kylie's song floated toward her:

"Clean, clean, clean my room.
Throw out all the trash.
Make the bed and sweep the floor and
Mom will give me cash."

It wasn't too hard for Megan to figure out that Mom had offered to pay Kylie to clean up her room; probably as a way to be certain Kylie would not bother her while she talked to her client.

Megan sighed. You would think by the age of six, Kylie either would have outgrown this singing habit or would at least use more than one tune.

"Do you have to sing the same song over and over?" Megan asked crossly.

"All my songs are different."

27

"The words are different but they're all the same melody: 'Row, Row, Row Your Boat.' "

"I *like* 'Row, Row, Row Your Boat.' "

"I don't. I'm sick of it."

"You don't have to listen."

Kylie lay on her stomach, reached under her bed, and dragged out a fistful of crayons. As she stuffed the crayons in the box she sang,

> *"Sing, sing, sing a song.*
> *Don't be still or lazy.*
> *Make up words to what you do,*
> *Drive your sister crazy."*

In spite of herself, Megan laughed. Although Kylie's songs *did* drive her crazy, she had to admire the way her sister could think up rhymes so quickly.

"How long is Mom going to be busy?" Megan asked.

Kylie shrugged. "A long time, I think. She said that after I clean my room I can watch our *Mary Poppins* video."

That was a bad sign. Mom rarely let either of the girls watch a movie until dinner was over and homework finished. It must be a really important client, and Mom must expect the call to take a long time.

Megan decided to return to the field and

copy down all the information from the sign. Maybe there would be a phone number to call. She could tell whoever answered the phone about the cats.

She put a small notepad and a pencil in the pocket of her windbreaker. Then she filled a plastic sandwich bag with cat food and put that in the other pocket. Even though she had already fed the cats once that day, Mommacat needed extra food right now.

Kylie wandered into the kitchen. "Why are you putting cat food in your coat?" she asked.

"It's for some stray cats." Megan started for the door.

"Can I go with you?"

"No."

"I want to see the cats."

"Not today," Megan said.

Kylie's lower lip stuck out. "You never let me go anywhere with you," she said.

That's because my ears get tired, Megan thought.

At the field, Megan refilled the food bowl and then went to the white sign. As she was copying the construction dates, a blue pickup truck pulled up to the curb beside her.

The man who was driving rolled down the

window and called to her. "What are you doing?"

He looked about Mrs. Perk's age, with dark hair that was thinning in front. He wore a denim work shirt with the sleeves rolled up.

"I'm writing down what the sign says." Megan mounted her bike as she spoke, uneasy about talking to a stranger. If he got out of the truck, she would ride away.

"Why?" he asked. He did not get out.

"It says someone plans to start building apartments here next week," Megan said. "But they can't do that."

"Why not?" he asked. "What's the trouble?"

"Some feral cats live in this field," Megan said. "I don't want them to be killed when the land is cleared. I bring them cat food and water every day."

The man frowned, clearly upset by what she said. "What kind of cats did you say?" he asked.

"Feral. You know, wild cats that live on their own. One of them is expecting kittens any day now. I'm going to call the company that put this sign up; maybe they will delay the apartment building until the cats can be caught."

"Cats!" the man said, as if he had never

heard of such an animal. He stepped on the gas and roared away.

Megan stared after the truck for a moment, puzzled by the man's odd reaction. Then she returned to copying the information from the sign. She had just finished when the blue truck returned.

Again the man spoke to her without getting out.

"It won't do any good for you to call," he said. "They'll never pay attention to a kid."

Megan was already worried about that. She was hoping Mom would call for her.

"I'll call the county building department," he continued. "I work in construction, so I deal with problems all the time; I know who to ask for."

"That would be great," Megan said. "I'll ask my mom to call, too, but I don't know when she'll have time to do it."

"Don't have her call. It's better to let one person handle it. I'll take care of it; don't worry."

He drove off again, and this time he did not return.

Megan was glad to have an adult concerned about the cats, but she wished she knew his name. How would she know what the people at the building department said?

What about the property owner and the

company who would be building the apartments? Someone should talk to them, too, and ask them to wait until the cats were rescued. She wished the man in the blue truck had not been in such a hurry.

Shane slammed his fist against the steering wheel as he drove away. Of all the rotten luck! Just when everything was going his way, some kid finds a bunch of cats living in the field. That's all he needed — some animal lover calling Brice and carrying on about homeless cats.

What if the media found out? He could imagine the headlines and the TV pictures of pathetic cats hiding in the weeds. Groups of picketers with SAVE THE CATS signs would show up, and some nut would chain himself to the bulldozer.

Shane pounded his fist on the wheel again as he imagined the scene. Then he took a deep breath, as he had been taught in the anger-management class the judge had made him take. He congratulated himself for thinking fast. He was sure the kid believed him when he said he would call the building department. All he had to do was keep her quiet for two days. That shouldn't be too hard.

Once the land was cleared, it wouldn't

matter how many cats used to live there. It would be too late to save them, and too late for the kid to keep the Evergreen Apartments from being built.

4

Lacey Wilcox gaped at her sister Danielle in astonishment. "How could you?" she demanded. "After what happened to Ben, how could you possibly steal anything?"

"I didn't think I'd get caught," Danielle mumbled.

"You didn't think, period." Lacey angrily slapped some peanut butter on a slice of bread, as if it were the sandwich's fault that her thirteen-year-old sister had been caught shoplifting.

"It wasn't really my fault," Danielle said. "My friends dared me to do it."

"Of course it was your fault." Lacey put the sandwich in her lunch bag, added a banana, and opened the cookie jar, hoping there might be a couple of Oreos left from the package she had brought home last night. No such luck.

"Mom's going to hit the roof," Danielle said.

"I don't blame her. Where was your

brain?" She put the packed lunch in the refrigerator, ready to take to school the next morning. She took out the last can of soda. Honestly she couldn't believe how her family ate everything she bought. She had put a six-pack of soda in there yesterday.

"Do you think I'll have to go to Juvenile Court, like Ben did?"

"Probably." Lacey rummaged in her shoulder bag for her car keys. "If you do, don't be a dope and smart off the way Ben did. Don't pretend it wasn't your fault. Just admit you were wrong, apologize, and promise you won't ever do it again." She headed for the door.

"Will you stay until Mom and Dad get home and tell them for me?" Danielle asked. "Please?"

"Sorry," Lacey said. "I have to go to work." Lacey started the engine and checked the gas tank. The needle was still above *empty;* she could buy gas after she got off work.

"Maybe I'll run away," Danielle said.

"Running away won't solve anything," Lacey said. "It would only get you in worse trouble."

"If I ran away, I wouldn't have to tell Mom and Dad."

"Look, Dani," Lacey said. "You goofed big time, but it isn't the end of the world. If you say you're sorry and mean it, you'll get another chance. I'll see you tonight."

Danielle's lip quivered, as if she would burst into tears any second. I can't help her with this, Lacey thought. She has to deal with it herself.

Lacey popped open her soda and took a sip as she drove off.

Sometimes Lacey thought she was the only one in her whole family who had any sense. At seventeen, Lacey was the fourth of five children and the first who planned to finish high school.

Her two older sisters both ran off with their boyfriends when they were sixteen. One got married and had two babies before she got a divorce at age nineteen. Now she worked as a maid in a motel. The other sister got hooked on drugs, moved to Los Angeles, and had not been heard from for over a year.

Lacey's brother, Ben, was currently in the county jail, serving six months for robbing a gas station. He had started shoplifting when he was ten and worked his way into bigger crimes. He was only two years older than Lacey, and this was his second time in jail.

And now Danielle. Lacey had talked to Dani about finishing school and making something of herself. Sure it was hard, especially when no one else cared whether you did it or not.

Lacey had started baby-sitting when she was twelve and saved every nickel she made. Then she got jobs weeding flower beds and raking leaves. By the time she was sixteen and could get a driver's license, she had saved enough money to pay for a car.

True, the car was fourteen years old and no beauty, but it enabled Lacey to get a real job, making decent money. Four evenings a week and all day on Saturday, Lacey was the hostess at Grogan's Restaurant. It was a nice restaurant, not a burger joint, where she got a share of the tips in addition to her salary.

Except for gas, car insurance, and her contributions to the family food supply, she saved her wages for college. No one in Lacey's family had ever gone to college, but she was going.

In two weeks she would graduate from Woodrow Wilson High School as valedictorian with the highest grade-point average of anyone in her class. She would receive a two-thousand-dollar academic scholarship from the Jefferson Foundation, and she had already been accepted in a work-study program at the community college. She would take nine credits each quarter and keep her job at Grogan's. All the years of hard work were about to pay off for Lacey.

Lacey sipped her soda, then put the can on the seat beside her. Danielle made her so angry. She mimicked her sister: "It wasn't really my fault." Whose fault was it, then? Nobody else put that lipstick in Dani's pocket.

As Lacey headed toward the freeway on-ramp, her thoughts on her younger sister, the can of soda tipped over. Lacey grabbed for it, hoping it wouldn't spill all over her skirt.

When she looked back at the street, she saw a minivan coming toward her from the right. She realized she and the minivan would reach the center of the intersection at the same time.

How did it get there so quickly? Had the driver run the stop sign? Or did I look away from the road too long?

Lacey slammed on her brakes, blasted her horn, and yanked the steering wheel to the left, trying to avoid a collision.

The other driver never slowed down.

In the split second before she hit the minivan, Lacey imagined everything she had worked for disappearing. An accident that was her fault would send her insurance costs through the ceiling. She would owe a big traffic fine, too. She'd never be able to afford college, even with the scholarship. She might even lose her driver's license, which would mean losing her job.

The cars collided. Lacey smelled the hot rubber from her tires as she stopped.

Looking back, she saw the minivan jump the curb and shudder to a stop in an empty field. It didn't roll over; it didn't crash into a tree or a telephone pole. Nobody was thrown out of it. She was sure the driver would be okay.

I don't need an accident in my life, Lacey thought. With my family history, the police might assume it was my fault whether it is or not, especially if the other driver is an adult. They'll probably think I was speeding, instead of just distracted.

With her heart thundering in her ears, Lacey stepped on the gas and roared up the on-ramp to the freeway.

Her hands shaking, she merged into the freeway traffic, then got off again at the next exit. She pulled into a parking lot, trembling all over now, and stopped the car.

Had anyone seen the accident? Were there witnesses who would be able to identify her car? If the police came and found her, she knew they would be harder on her than they would be if she went back now.

She replayed the accident in her mind. No cars had been on the on-ramp ahead of her, and when she looked in the rearview mirror, there hadn't been any cars behind her, either.

Remembering how the minivan plunged across the sidewalk, Lacey realized a person had been running through the field toward it. If the other driver needed help, someone was there.

She got out and examined her right front fender. The piece of plastic that covered the headlight was broken, and the fender was crumpled. But her car, including both front fenders, already had so many dents and dings that no one would ever notice this new damage unless she pointed it out to them.

It isn't as if I hit a person, Lacey told herself. Even to save her own future, she would never drive off and leave a person who needed help. She knew that she was making excuses; it was wrong to drive away from the accident, whether anyone was injured or not.

I can still go back, she thought. I can still admit to what I did, like I told Danielle to do.

She imagined the police giving her a ticket for reckless driving. She imagined herself selling her car, probably for less than she had paid for it, in order to pay the fine. She saw herself telling Mrs. Grogan, her boss, that she had to quit because she no longer had transportation. The bus was not an option; she had looked into that when she took the job, thinking it would be cheaper than driving. But she didn't get off work until eleven at night, and the next bus came at twelve-thirty and then stopped nearly a mile from Lacey's house.

She looked at her watch. If she hurried, she could still get to the restaurant on time.

She poured the rest of the soda onto the parking lot pavement. Then she started the car and headed for Grogan's.

5

Megan stood beside the white sign and watched the blue truck drive away. She knew it would not be easy to find homes for all the cats. They would need to be vaccinated against disease and neutered so they wouldn't keep having kittens. All of that would cost money, which Megan did not have. She had already spent three weeks' allowance on cat food.

She decided to ask Mom what to do. Even though Mom was busy, Megan knew she could count on her for help with something so important.

She moved slowly through the waist-high weeds toward the maple tree. If the cats were still eating, she didn't want to scare them away.

A spot of orange color in the weeds caught her eye. Pumpkin, his body hugging the ground and his ears flat, was watching her. Good, Megan thought. Maybe they're getting used to me. Maybe when it's time to catch them, they won't be so skittery.

As she reached the tree, she heard a loud screech of brakes. A horn honked. Megan looked toward the noise and saw a tan car slide through the intersection and smash into the side of a minivan. The crash of metal on metal was followed by glass showering to the pavement.

Pumpkin raced past Megan and up the tree.

The minivan veered toward the field, bumped over the curb and sidewalk, and lurched to a stop.

The tan car stopped briefly, then the driver accelerated.

As the car sped up the on-ramp toward the freeway, Megan caught a glimpse of the driver. She tried to get a license number, but the tan car was dirty, making the license plate hard to read, and the car was out of her sight before she could make out the numbers.

Megan rushed to the minivan to see if anyone needed help. The driver, a white-haired woman, did not move. The woman's head was thrown back and her eyes were closed, as if she had fallen asleep; her wrinkled hands still gripped the wheel.

There were no passengers.

Megan tried to open the driver's door, but

that side of the van was bashed in. The door no longer worked.

She knocked on the window. "Are you all right?"

The woman did not respond.

Other cars stopped. People hurried forward to help.

One man yelled, "I have a cell phone. I've called 9-1-1."

Megan ran around to the passenger side and was able to wrench that door open. A small gray dog leaped out. It had close-cropped fur and a stubby tail. Megan had not seen the dog when she looked in the window; it must have been on the floor.

The terrified dog took one look at Megan and at the people running toward the van, then dashed away into the weeds. Megan saw it run past the white sign and take off down the sidewalk. She hoped it wouldn't run into the traffic heading up the freeway on-ramp, but a frightened animal in unfamiliar territory might do anything.

"Are you all right?" Megan repeated. She leaned across the front seat and put one hand gently on the woman's arm.

There was still no reply.

"Help is on the way," Megan said. "Someone called an ambulance."

Other people crowded around the van,

asking questions, trying to open the driver's door.

"I'm a nurse," said a voice behind Megan. "Let me see her."

Megan gladly backed away and let the nurse take over.

I should try to catch the dog, Megan thought. It's bad enough that this woman was injured in an accident, without losing her dog, too. The poor dog must be scared to death.

Megan hurried across the field in the direction the dog had run. She saw no cats. Pumpkin was probably at the top of the maple tree by now, and no doubt the other cats had run off or hidden somewhere the minute the van roared into the field. She hoped Mommacat wasn't so frightened that she went somewhere else to have her babies.

Megan jumped on her bike and rode after the dog. She had ridden two blocks when she spotted the dog far ahead of her, still trotting down the sidewalk.

She heard the scream of a siren behind her; an ambulance was on its way.

Megan wondered why the driver of the tan car had not stopped. What if no one had seen the accident? What if nobody had been there to call 9-1-1 for the injured woman? Megan didn't understand how anyone could drive away after an accident, not knowing if the people in the other car were hurt or not.

Pedaling hard, Megan gradually gained on the dog. The sidewalk went under the freeway. Megan heard the rush of traffic above her and smelled the exhaust fumes.

On the other side of the freeway the scared dog dashed into a cross street. A horn honked. The dog kept running. When Megan reached the curb, she had to wait for three cars to pass before she could cross. Dog, she thought, you're lucky you aren't a fur pancake.

As they got farther from the freeway, the traffic noise subsided.

Megan wished she knew the dog's name. "Hey, doggie," she said. "Good dog." She figured most dogs who were family pets would know the words *good dog*.

The dog kept running.

Megan drew closer.

A mile beyond where the sidewalk went under the freeway, both the sidewalk and the street came to a dead end. A wire fence kept vehicles and pedestrians from going any further.

The gray dog flopped down beside the fence. His tongue hung out of his mouth. His sides heaved up and down.

Megan laid her bike down and walked slowly toward the exhausted animal. "Good dog," she said softly. "Good dog. I'm here to help you."

The dog raised his head and looked at her, but he did not get up.

Megan sat beside him. She closed her hand into a fist and held it toward the dog's nose. He sniffed briefly. Megan gently patted the dog's back. The dog rested his head on the ground again.

A tag dangled from the dog's collar. The tag read *Dinkle* and gave a phone number.

"Everything's going to be okay, Dinkle," Megan said. "I'll take you back to your mistress."

At the word *Dinkle,* the stubby tail wiggled.

Megan wished she had a leash, or even a piece of rope. The dog wore a collar, but she had nothing to attach to it. She was a long way from the field — much farther, Megan realized guiltily, than she was allowed to go by herself. She hadn't thought of that as she rushed after the dog.

She could leave her bike here and carry the dog all the way back, but she didn't want to do that. She had not brought the chain and padlock that she used when she rode her bike to school because she had not intended to be

47

away from her bike. What if someone stole it?

She wasn't sure she could carry the dog that far anyway; Dinkle would get heavy in a hurry. Or he might jump out of her arms and take off again.

Megan petted Dinkle some more and tried to think what to do.

Lacey tried to smile and act pleasant as she showed customers to their tables, but in her mind she went over and over the accident. It was completely her fault; there was no way around that. How could she have been so careless?

She had learned in Driver's Ed never to try to pick up a dropped item while she was driving. She knew better. Her mind had been on her sister when the soda spilled, but that was no excuse.

The restaurant phone rang while Lacey was seating a group in the private dining room. When she returned to her station, Mrs. Grogan said, "There's a call for you, Lacey. It's someone from the newspaper."

Lacey's heart leaped into her throat. "What do they want?"

Mrs. Grogan shrugged.

Lacey took a deep breath. Calm down, she told herself. How would the newspaper know anything about her involvement in the accident? Her voice trembled as she said, "Hello?"

"Lacey, it's Valerie from the *Daily Tribune*. I'm the one who interviewed you at school last week for the graduation story. I just wanted to let you know that the article and your photo will be in tomorrow morning's paper."

Lacey managed to say "thank you" before replacing the receiver. She had been thrilled when the journalist interviewed her and asked permission to print her senior class picture. Now it no longer seemed important.

6

After sitting beside the tired dog for a few minutes, Megan removed her windbreaker, zippered it shut, and slid one sleeve under the dog's collar. Then she tied the sleeves together at the wrists, pulling the knot as tight as she could.

Holding on to the bottom of her windbreaker, she stood up, letting the windbreaker act as a leash. She thought she could lead the dog this way and get him safely back to the field.

"Come on, Dinkle," Megan said. "You've rested long enough. It's time to head home."

When Megan tugged on the windbreaker, the dog stood and followed her.

It was awkward to walk her bike with one hand. It wobbled when she went up and down curbs in order to cross the streets. It took far longer to walk back to the field than it had taken her to ride her bike away from it.

By the time she returned to the wrecked

van, an ambulance had already taken the driver away.

Most of the people who had stopped to help or watch had left. A few stood in a group, talking about what had happened.

A helicopter circled the field; Megan knew it must be from one of the television stations.

Two police cars were parked near the white sign. The blue lights on top of the cars swirled around and around, making the sign look like an ad for a carnival ride.

Two officers searched the street where the accident had happened. A third directed traffic around the site. A woman carrying a large camera took pictures of the scene.

Another police officer walked toward the squad car.

Megan laid her bike down and hurried toward him. "This dog was in the wrecked van," she said. "After the accident, he jumped out and ran away. I went after him and caught him."

The woman immediately took a picture of Megan and the dog. Then she started scribbling in a notebook.

The officer introduced himself as Officer Rupp. He asked Megan questions about the dog. When he discovered that Megan had actually witnessed the accident, he wrote down her name, address, and phone number, then questioned her even more.

She told him everything she remembered. Yes, she had seen the car that drove away. Yes, she had seen the driver. No, she did not get a license number. Officer Rupp wrote her answers down.

The woman listened, too, making frequent notes.

"I may need to question you again," Officer Rupp said. "I'll call you if I do."

"All right."

"You can untie the dog now," Officer Rupp said. "I'll take him." He looked at the tag that hung from the dog's collar. "Dinkle?" he said. "What kind of crazy name is that?"

The dog wagged his tail.

"Hi, Dinkle," Officer Rupp said.

Dinkle wiggled all over and licked Officer Rupp's pant leg.

"What will you do with him?" Megan asked. "Do you know where he lives?" She knew it really wasn't her business, but she felt connected to the dog after chasing him and petting him and bringing him back to the field. She felt as if Dinkle was her friend.

"The driver was not able to talk," Officer Rupp said. "There was a name in her purse of who to call in an emergency, but no one answered. As soon as we can, we'll contact a family member or friend and tell them where to pick up the dog."

"Will you keep him with you until then?"

"He'll go to the county animal shelter."

"The shelter where the dog catcher takes strays?" Megan asked.

"We can't watch him at the police station, and we can't have him riding along in a squad car."

Megan looked down at Dinkle. She didn't want him to be locked in a cage at the animal shelter. He had been through enough.

"Could I keep him until you find out where he should go?" Megan asked. "He's getting used to me, and my mom won't care if I bring him home."

The policeman hesitated. "You're sure your mother will let you take him?"

Megan wasn't sure at all, but she thought she could talk Mom into it, especially since it would probably be for only a few hours. "Yes," she said. "He can stay in my room."

The officer reached down to pet the dog. "He'd be a lot better off with you," he said. "A day at the shelter and he'd be even more traumatized than he already is."

"Then I can take him home?"

Officer Rupp nodded. "I'll call as soon as I've talked to his owner or her family. Someone may come to pick him up yet today."

The woman handed Megan a business card. "I'm Amy Gleason from the *Daily Tribune*," she said. "Your picture will probably be in tomorrow morning's paper."

Megan grinned. She would call Chelsea tomorrow morning and tell her to be sure to read the newspaper.

When Megan got home, Kylie was drawing with chalk on the sidewalk in front of the house — and singing about it.

Megan interrupted the song. "Where's Mom?"

Kylie did not look up. "She's making dinner," she said, "and you're in trouble for being gone a long time and not telling her where you went."

"I'm a hero," Megan said. "My picture might be in the paper tomorrow morning."

Kylie quit drawing and looked at Megan. "Hey! Where did you get the dog? Do we get to keep him? What's his name? Why are you a hero?"

With Kylie chattering at full speed, Megan led the dog inside.

"Mom!" she called. "You won't believe what happened to me."

Mrs. Perk came out of the kitchen.

"Megan found a dog," Kylie said. "She's going to —"

"Hush, Kylie," Mrs. Perk said. "Let Megan tell it."

Megan did. She told about the screeching brakes and the crash and the injured driver. She told about the nurse who stopped to help, and about chasing the dog, and how she tied her windbreaker around Dinkle's collar. She told about the police and the journalist and how Dinkle was going to go to the county animal shelter unless Megan brought him home.

When she had finished, Mrs. Perk said, "Gracious, Megan, you are a one-person animal rescue society. First a bunch of cats, and now a dog. All in one week."

"The policeman said Dinkle would be better off here than at the animal shelter," Megan said. "Can I take care of him? It will only be for a short time."

"All right. I'll probably regret this, but we'll keep him here until his family comes to get him."

"Hooray!" Kylie shouted. "We get to keep Dinkle!"

"Only until his owner comes for him," Mrs. Perk said.

"Can he stay in my room?" Megan asked.

"No. We'll block off the kitchen and keep him in there where there's no carpet. He might not be house-trained."

Kylie threw her arms around the dog and began kissing his fur.

"Thanks, Mom," Megan said.

"I really should be angry with you," Mrs. Perk said. "You didn't leave a note; I had no idea where you were."

"I'm sorry. I only expected to be gone a few minutes. You see, I saw this sign about new apartments and I —"

Kylie began to sing.

> *"Pet, pet, pet the dog.*
> *Scratch him on the head.*
> *He can stay with us tonight*
> *Right beside my bed."*

"He's staying in the kitchen," Mrs. Perk said.

Dinkle walked away from her, toward the living room.

"Get the card table and block the doorway so he can't get on the carpet," Mrs. Perk said.

Megan did.

Dinkle whined.

"He's hungry," Kylie said. "He wants mashed potatoes and applesauce and chocolate pudding."

Megan knew those were Kylie's favorite foods.

"He's probably thirsty, after running so far," Mrs. Perk said.

Megan filled a bowl with water and put it on the floor. Dinkle lapped it eagerly, splashing water all around the bowl. Megan got a paper towel and wiped the floor. "What can I feed him?" she asked.

"He can have my green beans," Kylie offered.

"We'll go buy some dog food after we eat," Mrs. Perk said. "Get washed now; dinner's ready."

They had just finished eating when the telephone rang. Mrs. Perk answered. "Yes, officer," she said. "I can bring her to the station. When do you want us to come?"

Megan whispered to Kylie, "It's the police. They must want to talk to me some more."

But why? she wondered. I already told them everything I saw.

Mrs. Perk hung up and said, "The police want to talk to you again, Megan. I said I'd drive you to the station."

"Can I come?" Kylie asked. "Can we take Dinkle along?"

"Dinkle will stay here. We'll buy food for him on the way home." She picked up the phone again and asked the next-door neighbor, Mrs. Faber, if Kylie could come over for a visit, briefly explaining why.

Kylie howled in protest. "I want to go to the police station! It isn't fair!"

"I'm sorry, Kylie," Mrs. Perk said. "I don't know how long this will take. It's best for you to stay with Mrs. Faber."

Still protesting, Kylie went next door while Megan and her mother got in the car. As they drove off, they heard a mournful howl from the kitchen.

7

Officer Rupp met Megan and her mother at the police station.

After shaking hands with Mrs. Perk, Officer Rupp said, "I want you to tell me again, Megan, exactly what you saw."

Once more Megan told about the accident.

"What make of car was the tan car?" Officer Rupp asked.

"I don't know," Megan said.

"Was it new? Shiny?"

"It was old. The finish was dull, and there were some dents in it." She closed her eyes, trying to remember more details, but all she could recall was the sound of the crash and the shocking sight of the tan car speeding away.

"Did it have four doors or two?" Officer Rupp asked.

"Four, I think."

"Was there anyone in it, other than the driver?"

"I only saw the driver."

Officer Rupp gave Megan a sheet of paper that had a map of the accident area drawn on it. It showed the streets, the sidewalk, the freeway on-ramp, and the field.

"Please sketch for me where the cars were and where you were when you saw the accident," he said, handing Megan a pencil.

"I'm not very good at drawing," she said.

"Just use an *X* for one car and an *O* for the other. Show me which way they were going and where they were when they collided."

Megan drew the accident as well as she could. While she worked, her mother looked at the sheet of paper. "Exactly where did this accident take place?" Mrs. Perk asked.

Officer Rupp said, "At the on-ramp to Interstate 90, near the corner of 148th."

"At the field where the cats are," Mrs. Perk said.

Megan finished the drawing and explained it to Officer Rupp.

"Please tell me everything you can remember about the driver," he said.

"I only caught a glimpse of him."

"Hair color?"

"I didn't see his hair. He had on a cap." Megan had already said all this when Officer Rupp questioned her at the field. Why was he asking the same things again?

"Could you guess the driver's age?"

"Kind of young."

"How young? A teenager? Twenties?"

Megan shook her head. "I didn't see him well enough to be positive, but I think he was a teenager."

"What about skin color?"

Megan thought hard. "White. I'm sure he was white."

"Do you think you could describe him for a police artist? We'd like to try to get a drawing that resembles him."

Megan agreed to try.

The artist came and began questioning her. "Was his face long or round?"

"Sort of long."

To Megan's surprise, the artist drew on a computer rather than on paper. He showed Megan two sketches. "Did his eyes look like this — or more like this?"

"I saw him from the side, and only for an instant. I'm not sure about his eyes." Megan knew her answers were not useful, but she couldn't help it. In her mind, she had a faint idea of what the driver had looked like, but trying to put that fleeting glimpse into words was impossible. "His hair was kind of shaggy," she said, "as if he needed a haircut."

The artist kept asking questions and making changes in the sketch until finally

Megan said the drawing resembled the person she had seen. She knew the image still wasn't exactly right, but she didn't know what needed to be changed.

Officer Rupp thanked her for her help and then said, "If you remember anything else, no matter how unimportant it might seem, call me." He gave Mrs. Perk a business card. "This is my pager number. Call any time, day or night."

"Does the injured woman's family know about the dog yet?" Mrs. Perk asked.

"Not yet. Can you keep him overnight?"

"Yes. How is the woman? Have you talked to her?"

Officer Rupp shook his head. "She died soon after she arrived at the hospital."

"Oh no," Mrs. Perk said.

Megan got a sick feeling in her stomach. The woman she had tried to help, Dinkle's owner, was dead.

"That's why it's so important to find the other driver," Officer Rupp said. "This is no longer merely a hit-and-run accident, although that would be bad enough. The charge now could be vehicular homicide."

Megan stared in disbelief.

"We have not yet notified the victim's family," Officer Rupp said, "because we can't reach anyone. For now, I'd appreciate it if you did not talk to anyone about this."

"You do think the crash was accidental, don't you?" Mrs. Perk asked.

"Why do you ask that?"

Mrs. Perk looked sheepish. "I read a lot of detective novels," she said. "When an accident victim's spouse can't be found immediately, sometimes it turns out not to be an accident at all, and the spouse is guilty of murder."

"We're waiting for results of the autopsy to establish the cause of death," Officer Rupp said. "At this time we're looking into all possibilities."

On the way home, Megan and her mother stopped at the market. "Pick out some dog food," Mrs. Perk said. "I need to get a few other things. I'll meet you at the checkout counter."

Megan looked at the dozens of different kinds of dog food, unsure which one to choose. She finally selected a package with a picture of a dog that looked a little like Dinkle.

When they arrived home, Megan could hear Kylie singing a half block away. Looking toward the sound, she saw Kylie leading Dinkle on a leash. The neighbor, Mrs. Faber, walked with them.

Kylie bellowed, to her usual tune:

"Walk, walk, walk the dog
Up and down the street.
Scoop the poop and take it home.
Keep the sidewalk neat."

Megan couldn't believe her ears. There was her sister, happily carrying a little plastic bag full of dog-doo and singing about it at the top of her lungs. Megan hoped none of the other neighbors were listening.

"Mom!" Kylie shouted. "I took Dinkle for a walk!"

"Hush, Kylie," Mrs. Perk said. "Keep your voice down."

"I still had a leash," Mrs. Faber said, "from when I used to have Pepper. Dinkle was howling at being left by himself, so it seemed a good time to teach Kylie the proper way to walk a dog."

"She showed me how to use a bag to clean up after Dinkle," Kylie said. "All you do is —"

"Hush, Kylie!" Mrs. Perk repeated. She thanked Mrs. Faber and then instructed Kylie to put her bag in the garbage can.

Megan took Dinkle inside and fed him. He gobbled all the food and then put one paw in the empty bowl, to keep it from sliding across the floor while he licked it.

"Smart dog," Megan said. Dinkle wagged his tail.

After the dishes were done and Kylie had gone to bed, Mrs. Perk said, "We need to discuss those cats, Megan. I thought you weren't going to feed them anymore."

"We never finished talking about it," Megan said, "because you had to answer the phone. I planned to talk to you again as soon as I got home today but then I saw the accident and rescued Dinkle and everything got so confusing."

Megan's eyes filled with tears. "The most terrible thing has happened, Mom. All the cats are going to be killed unless I can save them."

"Calm down, Megan. Those cats are not going to be killed."

"Yes, they are!" Megan told her mother about the apartment building. "I had just copied the information from the sign when I saw the cars crash. The building is going to start next week."

"You won't be able to stop construction of the apartments," Mrs. Perk said. "The landowner has every right to build there."

"Maybe I can delay it until the cats are caught and taken somewhere else to live."

Mrs. Perk sighed. "Before you were born," she said, "when I dreamed of a daughter, I thought of tea parties and storybooks. Instead I got the police, a frightened dog, and a bunch of homeless cats in danger."

"We can't just let all those cats get bull-dozed," Megan said.

Mrs. Perk smiled at Megan. "No," she said, "we can't. It isn't their fault they have no home."

Megan let out her breath in relief. "What do you think I should do?" she asked.

"Call one of the groups who help animals, such as PAWS or the Humane Society. See if they will get involved. There's even one group called Feline Friends that does nothing but help homeless cats; I read an article about them recently. An organization will have a lot more clout than you will if you try to rescue the cats alone."

"That's a great idea."

"I'm afraid you're in for a big disappointment," Mrs. Perk said. "Even with help, it may be too late. Still, I'm glad my daughter is a compassionate person who wants to solve problems instead of just looking the other way."

"Is it okay if I keep feeding the cats until they're rescued? One of them is going to have kittens any time. She needs good food."

"All right. Just be careful. I don't want any more scratches."

"Thanks, Mom."

It wasn't until she was in bed that Megan

remembered the man in the blue truck, who had offered to call the building department. She had forgotten to tell Mom about him. Well, it didn't matter. Mom's suggestion to call the groups who help animals was a better idea anyway. They would know the right way to catch the cats, and where to take them.

8

Dinkle howled in the night. Megan got up twice to quiet him, but each time she left him alone, he immediately began howling again. The third time that Megan went to the kitchen, Mrs. Perk got up, too.

"He's lonesome," Megan said.

"Oh, all right," Mrs. Perk said. "Let him sleep on the floor beside your bed. None of us will get any rest if we leave him in the kitchen."

Dinkle did not stay on the floor. He curled up next to Megan, and she petted him until he fell asleep. After that, the only sound from Dinkle was a gentle snoring.

The next morning, Megan dressed quickly and brought in the *Daily Tribune*. She imagined the headline: YOUNG HEROINE RESCUES SCARED DOG. She wondered if it was too early to call Chelsea.

She flipped through the front section of the paper, looking for a picture of herself and Dinkle. It was not there. She went back through the paper more slowly and found the headline: POLICE SEEK DRIVER IN FATAL HIT-AND-RUN ACCIDENT.

The article said that a twelve-year-old girl who was feeding some feral cats in a nearby field had witnessed the accident, but it did not mention Megan's name. It didn't give the dead woman's name, either. Megan wondered if the woman's family knew yet. The article had a description of the tan car and a number to call if anyone had information about it. The artist's sketch was there, but it didn't look much like the driver Megan remembered. She wished she could have given a better description.

Disappointed not to find a picture of herself and Dinkle, Megan laid the paper on the table. She had expected to be a celebrity at school today. She had planned to cut her picture out of the paper and show it to all her friends.

The journalist, Amy somebody, had said she was going to use Megan's picture. Why had she changed her mind?

Megan fed Dinkle and took him for a walk. Afterward, while she ate her breakfast, she looked in the telephone directory. She wrote down the numbers of three agencies that help animals.

She tried Feline Friends first but got a

message saying that the office opened at nine o'clock. It was too early. She got similar messages when she tried PAWS and the Humane Society.

She didn't want to explain the situation on voice mail, so she left no messages. She would call after school.

She hoped one of the agencies would be willing to help the cats. If they weren't, Megan wasn't sure what she would do.

Shane shifted in his chair at the county building department, waiting for his number to be called. He needed to be sure that nothing would hold up the construction of the apartment complex.

"There has been no opposition to the project," the clerk said, when it was finally Shane's turn. "Unless there's a last-minute problem, you can pick up the building permit tomorrow."

A last-minute problem, Shane thought, such as a bunch of wild cats with no place to go.

Shane hurried out to his truck. There would be no last-minute problem, no reason for Brice to delay clearing the field. Shane would see to that.

On Friday morning, Shane would drive to Elmwood and cash the forged check and close out his savings account.

With luck, he would sell his truck by Friday, too. His ad was already running in *Auto Trader*, and two people had called about it.

He would fly the Colby hot-air balloon and stage the crash-and-burn "accident" Friday night, then head for New Mexico.

Once the apartment project was started, the money Shane had stolen would not be missed until the end of June, when the bookkeeper figured the quarterly business taxes. Maybe not even then.

If the theft was discovered, Brice would never accuse Shane because by then Brice would think Shane was dead.

Everything was working out exactly as Shane had hoped. All he had to do was keep the kid quiet about the cats. That should be a piece of cake.

That afternoon, Megan hurried home from school. She planned to walk Dinkle, feed the cats, and then start telephoning the animal agencies.

As she approached her house, she heard her sister's song coming from the end of the block.

"Walk, walk, walk the dog
Up and down the street. . . ."

Good, Megan thought. Kylie's taking care of Dinkle. That will save me some time.

She took her homework out of her backpack and put the cat food and the jar of fresh water in. Then she wrote a quick note to her mother, got on her bike, and took off before Kylie could see her and beg to go along.

The smashed van was gone. Megan did not go to the place where it had been. It gave her a strange feeling to know that yesterday at this time, a woman had died there. Although she had never met the woman, Megan felt sad.

She walked quietly toward the tree where she had left the dish of cat food yesterday. She looked from side to side as she walked, hoping to catch a glimpse of Mommacat.

At the base of the tree, Megan saw a package the size of a shoe box, wrapped in plain brown paper. Someone had written on the paper with a red marker: CAT FOOD.

That's odd, Megan thought. Had someone seen her feeding the cats and wanted to help? But why do it this way? Why not just put the cat food in the dish?

She picked up the package; it was too light to be full of cat food. She removed the wrapping paper and opened the box. Inside was a sheet of white paper, with a message written in the same red marker.

*If you want the cats to live, don't tell anyone.
You are the only one who knows. Keep it that
way.*

There was a P.S. at the bottom of the page. It said: *Do not show* anyone *this note.*

Megan read the message a second time. *If you want the cats to live, don't tell anyone.*

Don't tell anyone what? About the accident?

She put the note in her pocket, then stuffed the box and the wrapping paper in her backpack.

She poured fresh water in the cats' bowl and filled the pie plate with cat food.

She took out the paper and read the message again.

The note must be from the driver of the tan car, Megan thought. He thinks I can identify him and wants to scare me so I won't do it. He knows from the newspaper article that I come here to feed the cats, so he knew where to leave his message.

She had already told the police everything she remembered about the driver. It was too late for anyone to warn her not to tell. Of course, the driver didn't know that.

Her hands trembled as she folded the note and put it in her pocket. The driver must be desperate to write such a threatening note. Maybe Mom was right. Maybe the crash had not been an accident.

A new idea exploded in Megan's mind. If the crash was on purpose, she thought, then I am the only witness to a murder! Now the murderer is threatening to kill all the cats if I tell the police about him, or about this note.

Megan swallowed hard. She remembered that Officer Rupp had told her not to talk about what she had seen.

She wondered if the police had feared some sort of threat. Maybe that was why her picture wasn't in the paper. Maybe the police had told the newspaper not to use Megan's name because she was the only one who had seen the tan car, and they didn't want the driver to know who she was.

The driver had found her anyway, even without knowing her name.

Megan debated what to do. Should she call Officer Rupp and tell him about the note?

How would the person who left the note know whether Megan told anyone about it or not? Was someone watching her?

Megan looked quickly around. Two cars headed up the freeway on-ramp; neither was tan. There was no car parked near the field, and no one was walking nearby.

"Mew." The soft sound broke in to

Megan's thoughts. "Mew, mew." It came from the drainpipe.

Megan knelt in the grass and looked inside the drainpipe. She couldn't tell for sure how many kittens there were, but several tiny bodies squirmed and mewed next to Mommacat. They were so small, they looked more like mice than kittens.

Megan longed to pick up one of the kittens, but she knew better than to reach inside the drainpipe. Mommacat would surely try to protect her babies. The scratch on Megan's hand had finally begun to heal, and she didn't want another one.

Megan brought the pan of food and the bowl of water closer, leaving them just outside the drainpipe.

The kittens helped Megan decide what to do about the note. Taking it to the police would not help the woman who had died. Even if Megan could identify the driver of the tan car, which she could not, it wouldn't bring back Dinkle's owner.

But it was not too late to help the cats. These new little kittens could be caught and tamed. They could be adopted by people who would love them and care for them. They wouldn't have to grow up hungry and fearful and wild, as Mommacat and the others had.

Megan decided not to tell anyone about the note until all the cats had been safely moved to new homes. Then she would show the note to Mom and call the police.

She peered in the drainpipe at the newborn kittens one more time before she walked to her bike. She needed to get going or it would be too late to call Feline Friends. Their office was only open until four-thirty.

As Megan got on her bike, the same blue pickup truck came down the street and stopped beside her.

The driver rolled down his window and called, "Good news! I found out who owns the land. I'll call the owner and ask him to pay for relocating the cats."

"That's great!" Megan said.

"We should have his answer by Tuesday. In the meantime, the county has put the building permit on hold. Your cats are safe for at least a month."

"I'm going to call a group called Feline Friends," Megan said. "They help homeless cats. They might know a place where the cats can live."

The man's smile disappeared. "Don't call them until I've contacted the property owner," he said. "Feline Friends would need his permission to remove the cats, since they are on private property. This situation could get a lot of publicity, and the property owner is more likely to cooperate if he knows what's going on before the media gets wind of it."

"All right," Megan said. "I won't call them yet. But how will I know if the owner is going to help or not?" She thought of giving this man her phone number but decided it wasn't smart to do that when she didn't really know him.

"I drive past here several times daily. I'll watch for you. If I don't see you, call me on Tuesday."

He took a business card from his wallet. He opened the truck's glove compartment and reached inside for a pencil. He crossed out the telephone number on the card and wrote down a different number. Then he handed the card to Megan.

It read:

COLBY CONSTRUCTION
Brice Colby, *President*

"Thanks for your help, Mr. Colby," Megan said.

The man waved and drove away.

Megan wondered why Mr. Colby was being so helpful. Maybe he just likes cats, she decided. Maybe he has a cat of his own.

Now she didn't need to hurry home to call Feline Friends or the other animal-welfare agencies. She could stay and watch for Mommacat to come out of the drainpipe and eat. She could make sure Mommacat and her kittens were okay.

In her relief at having help with the cat problem, she forgot for a moment about the note in her pocket.

9

Lacey bought a morning newspaper on her way to school the morning after the accident. She skimmed it quickly until she found the headline: POLICE SEEK DRIVER IN FATAL HIT-AND-RUN ACCIDENT.

Fatal? Disbelief slid down Lacey's backbone. It must be a different accident. *Fatal* meant someone had died. She had not hit the other car hard enough for anyone to be killed. Had she?

As Lacey read the whole article, her breathing became shallow and rapid. It was her accident, no doubt of that. An autopsy was being done to determine the exact cause of death.

The only witness to the accident, a twelve-year-old girl, had been in the empty field feeding some feral cats.

A sketch of the missing driver accompanied the story. Lacey didn't think the sketch looked anything like her. For one thing, the witness had thought she was a boy. Also, the person in the sketch had a long face and high cheekbones; he looked older than Lacey, and thinner.

No one who sees that sketch will think of me, Lacey thought. Will they?

Feeling sick to her stomach, Lacey quit reading and looked behind her, as if fearing her parents and teachers and all her friends were reading the article over her shoulder.

I should have stopped right away, she thought. Or I should have turned around and gone back instead of continuing on to Grogan's. If I had stopped, maybe I could have helped that woman.

She wondered what would happen if she turned herself in now. Maybe she would be sent to the county jail, just like her brother. Maybe worse. Maybe a federal prison. When you kill somebody in an accident, and don't stop to help them, is it the same as murdering them? Lacey didn't know and she didn't want to find out.

Could the girl identify me, if she saw me? Lacey wondered. Lacey didn't think so. If the girl had seen Lacey clearly, the sketch in the paper would resemble her more closely.

Lacey was positive the girl had not seen Lacey's license plate. If she had, the cops would have come by now.

Lacey was sorely tempted to skip school

and hide out somewhere. She wanted to be alone. She could call the school office and say she felt sick, which was the truth. She could hang out at the mall or go to the public library and study.

But she had her final exam in algebra that day, and she needed an *A* to maintain her average.

Besides, if anyone thought that she was involved in the hit-and-run accident, it would look mighty suspicious if she was not at school the day after the accident happened.

No, she would sit in class as usual, and take her test, and try to act normal. After school she would go to work, just as she did every day, although she would drive a different route so she didn't have to pass the scene of the accident. Lacey didn't think she would ever again be able to drive past that corner.

She would go on with her life as if nothing had happened, and hope against hope that no one ever found out what she had done. Because if they found out, everything she had worked for all these years was out the window. She was sure the Jefferson Foundation did not give scholarship money to drivers who kill someone, accidentally or not, and then leave the scene.

No scholarship meant no college, just as

no car meant no job. She would end up like the rest of her family — doing time behind bars or cleaning toilets in a motel.

It wouldn't do the dead woman any good to have Lacey turn herself in now. All that would happen if she confessed was that two lives would be ruined because of the accident instead of one — the dead woman's and her own.

Lacey stuffed the newspaper into the trash container outside the school and started for her first class.

Mommacat stayed in the drainpipe with her kittens. Megan finally grew tired of waiting for her and went home. She found Kylie sitting morosely on the front steps.

"Dinkle's gone," Kylie said, her eyes brimming with tears. "A man came and got him."

"Who?" Megan said.

"Mr. Leefton. His mother got killed in that accident you saw."

"When did he come?"

"A little while ago," Kylie said. "He talked to Mom on the phone before he came. He was out of town yesterday and didn't find out what had happened until ten o'clock. He thought that was too late to call us, and he was too upset last night, anyway."

Megan was glad that there was a reason

why the police had been unable to reach the family sooner. It meant that Megan had not witnessed a murder; the crash really had been an accident. Somehow the note in her pocket didn't seem quite as threatening if the collision was accidental.

"Was Dinkle glad to see him?" Megan asked.

Kylie wiped her eyes on the sleeve of her sweatshirt. "Dinkle went nuts! He yipped and jumped and ran around in circles."

"Good," Megan said.

"Mr. Leefton wasn't happy, though," Kylie said. "He cried. But then he kneeled down and hugged Dinkle, and then he blew his nose and was okay."

Megan felt sorry for Mr. Leefton; it would be awful to have your mother die.

"Dinkle kept licking Mr. Leefton's hand," Kylie said.

Megan was glad Mr. Leefton and Dinkle were together. They probably needed each other right now. She wished she had been home when Mr. Leefton came. "Did Mom tell him how I chased Dinkle and caught him?" she asked.

"Yes. And I told him how I walked Dinkle and cleaned up after him. I was going to sing my walk-the-dog song for him, but Mom told me to hush."

"I can't imagine why."

"He tried to give me twenty dollars for taking care of Dinkle, half for you and half for me, but Mom wouldn't let me take it."

"That's okay," Megan said. "I wouldn't want to take a reward for helping Dinkle."

"I would," Kylie said. She started to cry again. "I wanted to keep Dinkle."

"He wasn't ours."

"I wanted to keep him anyway. I already had a song made up for when I play ball with him." She began to sing, "Throw, throw, throw the ball —"

Megan interrupted. "One of the cats I feed had kittens today," she said. "I'm going to ask Mom if I can keep one of them."

Kylie brightened. "Can I keep one, too? If we had two kittens, they could play together and not be lonesome when we're at school. Being lonesome isn't any fun."

The wistful tone of Kylie's voice told Megan that her sister was not referring only to the kittens.

"You can ask Mom," Megan said.

"If I get a kitten," Kylie said, "I'm going to name it Dinkle."

Megan went inside to get a snack. The morning paper was still on the kitchen counter. Megan glanced at it as she reached for a banana.

She paused and looked more closely. It was a different section of the paper than the one she had read that morning. The article was about high school seniors and their plans for next year.

But it wasn't the article that caught Megan's eye; it was one of the photos.

It's him, Megan thought. It's the driver of the tan car! Only it isn't a boy, it's a girl. The girl's hair was cut short; Megan could see why she had thought the driver was a boy.

She read the paragraph that accompanied the photo. Lacey Wilcox, she learned, was the fourth of five children and would be the first in her family to graduate from high school. She was valedictorian, with a 3.98 grade point average, and planned to attend the community college next fall.

This can't be the driver, Megan thought. A girl smart enough to have the best average in her whole class would never leave the scene of an accident. She certainly would never leave me a note threatening to kill the cats.

And yet — a girl like that had a whole lot to lose if anyone discovered she had caused a wreck. Maybe she was scared that she would get an expensive traffic fine or that her driver's license would be canceled. Would she be scared enough to drive away from the accident and, later, to write a menacing note?

Maybe Lacey Wilcox had a brother or a cousin who looked like her. Maybe that's who was driving the tan car when the accident happened.

Maybe.

Megan studied the photo again and knew in her bones that it was not a brother or a cousin. She had seen the driver for such a brief time, and yet there was a definite likeness. If the police artist had sketched this photo, Megan would have said, yes, that's exactly right. That's the hit-and-run driver.

Megan knew she should call Officer Rupp and tell him that the newspaper photo looked like the driver of the tan car.

But what if she turned Lacey Wilcox in, and then Lacey did what she had said she would do? Anybody who was desperate enough to write a threatening note and wrap it up in a box labeled CAT FOOD was capable of most anything, including killing the feral cats.

Megan couldn't take a chance on that.

She fingered the note in her pocket. She didn't have to remove it to remember what it said. "If you want the cats to live, don't tell anyone."

I *do* want them to live, Megan thought, all

of them: Pumpkin and Twitchy Tail and Claws and Slush and Mommacat and the new little kittens. They would all be safe in a few days, as soon as Mr. Colby made the arrangements.

After the cats are out of the field, Megan thought, I'll tell the police that I know who was driving the tan car.

She got a pair of scissors and clipped the picture and the article about Lacey Wilcox out of the newspaper. As soon as the cats were safely in their new homes, she would show the photo to Officer Rupp.

She would show him the note then, too. But not now.

Kylie skipped into the kitchen. "Mom says maybe," she said.

Mrs. Perk followed Kylie. "I hear your mother cat had her kittens," she said, "without any help from you."

"I couldn't tell how many there were," Megan said. "She had them in a drainpipe. I hope it doesn't rain soon; they'll get soaked if it does."

"That mother cat will move them to a dry place if it rains," Mrs. Perk said.

"How soon can we bring the kittens home?" Kylie asked.

"Kittens need to stay with their mother for six weeks," Mrs. Perk said. "Then we'll see."

"They're free," Megan pointed out. Mom always liked a bargain.

"Free cats need to get their shots," Mrs. Perk replied. "They'll have to be wormed, and we'll need to buy food and a litter box."

"I'll help pay," Megan said. "I can use my birthday money."

"I have sixteen cents," Kylie said.

"We don't even know if these kittens will be healthy enough to adopt," Mrs. Perk said. "Did you call Feline Friends?"

"No," Megan said. "I met a man who wants to save the cats, too, and he is going to call the property owner to ask him to help. He told me not to call Feline Friends until the owner is notified."

Mrs. Perk frowned. "What man?" she asked. "Where did you meet him?"

"He was driving by when he saw me copying the information from the sign, and he stopped and asked what I was doing."

"Megan, you know you shouldn't talk to strangers."

"I was careful, Mom. He didn't even get out of his truck. He gave me his business card with his name and telephone number on it. He already got the county to put a hold on the building permit until the cats get moved."

Mrs. Perk looked unconvinced.

Megan got the man's business card and handed it to her mother.

"Brice Colby?" Mrs. Perk said. "This is who's helping you?"

"Do you know him?"

"He and his wife belong to my book club. Our group met at their home twice last year."

"He seemed nice," Megan said, "and he offered to help."

"You can count on Brice to get things done," Mrs. Perk said. "If Brice Colby says he'll help you save those cats, you don't have a thing to worry about."

That night as Megan tried to fall asleep she remembered Mom's words: You don't have a thing to worry about.

Not a thing, Megan thought as she stared into the dark, except the fact that I'm withholding information from the police about a driver who left the scene of an accident. Plus I have a note from the driver, saying she'll kill all the cats if I tell the police who she is.

10

Megan slept fitfully. She dreamed of car crashes, and of cats that multiplied until there were thousands of them, all wailing from hunger, and of strange notes written with red marker in a foreign language that she couldn't read.

At breakfast Mrs. Perk said, "Be sure you're home by four-thirty this afternoon. We need to leave for the balloon festival by five, or we'll never find a place to park, and I want to eat dinner before we go."

"We can eat after we get there," Kylie said. "Last year they sold cotton candy and ice-cream cones and caramel corn."

"We are not eating junk for dinner," Mrs. Perk said.

"Can we buy cotton candy for dessert?" Kylie asked.

"Cotton candy is pure sugar," Mrs. Perk said.

"I know," Kylie said. "That's why I like it. Please, Mom?"

"We'll see."

"If they have pink and blue," Kylie said, "I'm going to get pink, and I'm going to eat it without using my fingers."

"Your face will be a sticky mess," Megan said.

Kylie began to sing:

> *"Take, take, take a bite*
> *Of my cotton candy.*
> *Let it melt inside my mouth.*
> *Sugar tastes just dandy."*

Megan rolled her eyes as she put cat food and the jar of fresh water in her backpack. She would go straight to the field after school, to feed the cats and check on the kittens.

She was glad it was Friday. She looked forward to the weekend. Today she would have to hurry to the field and then hurry home to go to the balloon festival. Tomorrow and Sunday she could stay at the field and watch Mommacat and her babies. Maybe her friend Chelsea would be well and able to come with her. Tomorrow she planned to take Mommacat a can of tuna, for a special treat.

Shane Turner worked until noon on Friday. He left on his lunch break as if it were any ordinary day, but he knew it was not ordinary at all.

He walked toward his truck, knowing he would never return. He had worked his last hour for Colby Construction Company. His plan was now in progress.

After he ate, Shane drove fifty miles north to the bank he had chosen because they advertised "small-town friendliness." He had opened a savings account there as William Bradburn soon after he began working for Brice. Each week after he cashed his paycheck at the bank where he was known as Shane Turner, he had deposited some cash in Mr. Bradburn's account. With interest, he now had over two thousand dollars.

The teller recognized him, and that was okay because by the time his true identity was known, everyone would think he was dead.

"I need to close my account," he said, "and also cash a check. I'm moving out of the area."

The teller asked to see Shane's driver's license, because the check was so large. She copied down the number.

Shane smiled as the bank teller counted out thousand-dollar bills, put the cash in an envelope, and handed it to him.

"Is there anything else I can do for you,

Mr. Bradburn?" the teller asked.

"No, thanks," Shane said.

He put the envelope in the pocket of his leather jacket and zippered the pocket shut.

He felt giddy as he walked to his truck. Imagine having seventeen thousand dollars in his pocket! Even when he robbed the bank in White Springs, he had carried away less than six thousand. Of course he didn't get to keep that money because he got caught just four blocks from the bank. This time he was smarter; this time he would not get caught.

As soon as he was inside the truck, he locked the doors. He needed to be careful. There are a lot of dishonest people in the world.

Shane drove to his apartment, where he was supposed to meet a man who had answered Shane's ad about a truck for sale. Shane would sell the blue pickup even if he had to come down in price. He had already told the prospective buyer that it had to be a cash sale.

While he drove, Shane mentally walked through the rest of his day. As soon as his truck was sold, he would take a bus to the airport, where the balloon festival was held.

When it was time for him to fly the hot-air balloon sponsored by Colby Construction, there would be a problem. The balloon would rise into the sky at dusk with the other balloons in his part of the demonstration, but instead of hovering over the runway for a short time and then landing again, as it was supposed to do, Shane's balloon would keep going. It would not come back. Not ever.

He knew Brice would try to call him on the cellular phone that was in the balloon's basket to ask what was wrong and to keep track of the balloon's location. Shane, of course, did not intend to turn the phone on.

During scheduled balloon flights there was always a chase car at hand to follow the balloon on the ground. Tonight the chase car would not be there, since no flight was expected. After dark, the balloons at the festival gave demonstration rides, going up only a short distance and returning. The longer flights would be the next day.

By the time anyone on the ground could get in a car to try to follow the wayward balloon tonight, Shane would be over the top of Desolation Hill and out of sight. He would land long before the chase car could drive around the hill and spot the balloon.

Shane had practiced flying the same route several times in the past month. He had used the Colby Construction balloon, telling Brice he wanted to practice for the festival.

He knew the air currents; he knew exactly how much gas to give the balloon to get it high enough to go over the hill. The winds had been calm all week and no storms were predicted, so there was nothing to prevent him from taking off as planned.

His landing place wasn't far, as the crow flies, but on the ground it was a slow, winding drive on a rarely used loggers' road. The airport was at the edge of town, and the hills beyond, leading to the Cascade Mountains, were unpopulated.

With any luck even the flames, when he set the balloon on fire, would not be seen. The balloon might not be found for months, or even years.

Everyone would think his balloon had crashed. When Shane wasn't found, he would be presumed dead.

Eventually the charred remains of the balloon and basket would be discovered — probably by hikers or hunters. By then, of course, Shane would be long gone to New Mexico, using his new name. He would search for a balloon to buy. He was ready to have his own business.

Filled with dreams of his life in New Mexico, Shane parked in front of his apartment and waited for the prospective truck buyer to arrive.

An hour later, as the new owner of the blue pickup drove away, Shane added eighteen hundred dollars to the envelope in his pocket. One more part of his plan had gone exactly as he had envisioned it.

Shane thought how close that girl and her wild cats had come to ruining all of his plans. If he had not been able to keep her quiet about the cats, the apartment project would have been delayed. Without that huge project to generate money for Colby Construction, a missing fifteen thousand dollars would likely be noticed.

Shane was positive that if Brice had known about the cats, he would have delayed the apartments. Brice and Ruthann treated their own pets like members of the family. Shane had no doubt that Brice would have postponed clearing that field, even if it meant a financial loss. He shook his head at his brother-in-law's stupidity.

Shane looked at the time. Two o'clock. The bulldozer driver should be nearly done. By five o'clock the field would be leveled, so it didn't matter what Brice would have done. Brice would never know about the cats.

Shane smiled at his own brilliance. He

had kept the girl from telling. He had pre-
vented her from ruining his plans. By now
the field was cleared and her precious cats
were in Kitty Heaven.

Lacey's little sister was waiting for her
when Lacey got home from school on
Friday. "I did what you told me to do,"
Danielle said. "I paid for the lipstick and
told the store manager I was sorry and
would never take anything again."

"Good for you," Lacey said. "What did he
say?"

"He said he'd drop the charges. I don't
have to go to juvenile court." Danielle
grinned. "You were right," she said. "It's
better to face up to a mistake than to run
away from it."

Too bad I don't take my own advice,
Lacey thought. It was two days now since
the accident, and she was more nervous and
upset about it than she had been the day it
happened.

She might still get caught; the cops had all
sorts of ways of tracking people down. She
remembered a news report of how a broken
filament from a headlight had alerted inves-
tigators what kind of car to look for.

The longer it was between the accident
and the time they found her, the worse it

would be for her. She knew that. She knew she should do what Danielle had done and face up to her problem — but she couldn't make herself do it.

Only a fool would risk losing a college scholarship and a job and an opportunity for a good life if she didn't have to. If she kept her mouth shut, there was a good chance no one would ever know about her role in the fatal accident.

The trouble was, she felt like such a creep. Even if she never got caught, she still felt like a creep.

I was involved in that woman's death, Lacey thought, and I don't even have the decency to tell her family that I'm sorry. Can I live with that for the rest of my life?

11

Megan hurried out of school on Friday afternoon, hopped on her bike, and headed for the field. Although she knew the balloon festival would be fun, she wished she didn't have to go home early. She wanted to watch the kittens.

When she was a block away, she saw a large flatbed truck parked at the front edge of the field, near the sign. For a second, she thought maybe Mr. Colby was waiting for her in a different kind of truck. Then she saw a big yellow bulldozer on the far side of the truck.

Megan's heart, and her feet, pumped faster.

Just as she reached the field, the bulldozer's engine started. She flinched at the sudden loud noise.

A man sat in the cab part of the bulldozer.

"Hello!" Megan called, as she rode toward the bulldozer. "Hello! I need to talk to you!"

The machine's large steel treads crawled

away from the flatbed truck, rolling forward and under like metal conveyor belts as they moved the bulldozer toward the edge of the field that adjoined the freeway on-ramp.

The driver, intent on steering the machine, kept his eyes straight ahead.

This can't be happening, Megan thought, as she dropped her bike in the weeds and ran toward the bulldozer.

The engine noise rumbled like thunder.

"Stop!" Megan shouted. "Stop!"

The driver still did not look at her.

He can't hear me over the roar of the bulldozer, Megan realized.

When the front edge of the bulldozer's treads crossed the sidewalk, the machine paused. Then the driver backed the dozer into position so that its scoop would come down right along the edge of the sidewalk.

Halfway between the bulldozer and the other end of the field, Megan saw the drainpipe. Its opening was only a few feet from the sidewalk. Megan's stomach felt as if she had swallowed a brick.

Would the scoop fill the drainpipe with dirt as it passed, trapping Mommacat and the kittens inside the pipe? Or would the frightful noise as the bulldozer approached drive Mommacat to try to carry her kittens to safety? If so, they would never make it.

Megan raced toward the bulldozer. Her worst fear for the cats was about to come true.

"Stop!" she screamed. "You can't do this!"

She reached the bulldozer just as the driver pulled a lever that lowered the scoop to the ground. She saw that the driver wore earphones to protect him from the constant noise of the huge machine. It didn't matter how loud Megan shouted; the driver would never hear her.

She ran in front of the bulldozer and stopped about ten feet before the scoop. She waved her arms frantically. Even though she knew the driver could not hear her, she continued to yell, "Stop! Stop!"

The driver shifted another lever. The bulldozer's blade dug into the dirt, then started to push it forward.

Megan jumped up and down, desperately flailing her arms. She saw the driver glance up; he had an astonished look on his face. She knew he had seen her.

The bulldozer quit moving. The engine stopped. The driver stood up, removed his earphones, and leaned out of the cab.

"What's the matter with you? Are you crazy?" he said. "Get out of the way!"

Megan rushed to the side of the bulldozer and looked up at the man. "You aren't supposed to clear this field," she said.

"Is that so? Then why did I get a call telling me to be sure it gets done today?"

"There's been a mistake," Megan said.

"There's no mistake. This is the corner of 148th and I-90, and I'm supposed to clear it."

"But you can't!" Megan said.

"Look," the driver said. "I'm sorry if this field is where you like to play. I'm sorry if you don't want an apartment building to go up here. But I don't make those decisions; all I do is drive my 'dozer. I promised I'd have this land leveled by five o'clock this afternoon, and I'm already three hours late getting started because I got held up on a different job."

"There are cats living in this field," Megan said. "The clearing is not supposed to be done until the cats are caught and moved to a new place."

"Cats?" The driver looked at her as if she had started speaking a language he didn't understand.

"Feral cats. One of them has a litter of new kittens."

"I don't know about any cats. All I know is I'm supposed to do a job here this afternoon. So you need to stay out of my way where you won't get hurt, and let me get on with it."

Megan took a deep breath, trying to keep her voice from shaking. "If you start clearing this field," she said, "I will call the television hot-line number for breaking news."

"What?"

"I'll tell the TV reporter that you are bulldozing a field that is not supposed to be cleared, and that your bulldozer is killing all the cats. The cameras will be here within minutes."

"Whoa," the man said. He took off his cap and scratched the side of his head.

"Do you really want to be on the ten o'clock news in a story about how you murdered a litter of baby kittens?"

The man climbed down off the bulldozer. "Maybe I should call my boss and double-check this job order," he said. "Mr. Colby didn't set this up himself the way he usually does. Someone else called me."

"Mr. Colby?" Megan asked. "From Colby Construction? Is he your boss?"

"That's the one."

Relief flowed through Megan. "Mr. Colby will tell you not to clear this field," she said. "He's helping me save the cats. He even got the county to withhold the building permit on these apartments for a month."

The driver looked skeptical. "I find that hard to believe," he said. "No contractor would deliberately hold up his own building permit, cats or no cats. Why would he do that?"

"So there would be time to move the cats to new homes before the land gets cleared."

"You don't need a building permit in order to clear the land."

"You don't?" Megan said.

"No, you don't," the driver said. "Besides, Brice Colby is the one who's building these apartments. If he wants to postpone construction, all he has to do is wait."

"Are you sure Colby Construction is building these apartments?"

"That's who called and told me to get over here today. But I'll call Mr. Colby and get his okay before I continue."

Megan followed the man to the flatbed truck and waited while he unlocked it and took out a cellular phone. He dialed, then asked for Brice Colby.

After a pause he said, "This is Dale Burrows. I'm supposed to be clearing for the Evergreen Apartments this afternoon, and I have a problem on the job site. I need to talk to Brice as soon as possible." He gave a phone number.

He hung up and told Megan, "His office is going to page him on his beeper and ask him to call me."

She hoped Mr. Colby called promptly. She was supposed to be on her way home by now. Mom would not be happy if Megan was late today.

"I'm going to put out the cats' food and water while we wait," Megan said.

Carrying his cell phone, the bulldozer driver followed her. He watched while Megan filled one dish with cat food and the other with fresh water. "How many cats are you feeding here?" he asked.

Megan held up one finger for each name. "Pumpkin, Slush, Twitchy Tail, Claws, and Mommacat. That's five, for sure, but there may be some I haven't seen. Plus the kittens. I don't know yet how many of those there are."

As they talked, Megan glanced around to see if anyone might be watching. She hoped whoever had left the note didn't think she was telling this man about the accident.

"Do you want to see the kittens?" she asked.

"Why not?" the driver said.

She knelt and peered inside the drainpipe. "There they are," she said, "but don't try to touch them."

The driver looked into the drainpipe. "They're tiny," he said. "How old are they?"

"They were born yesterday. As soon as

they're six weeks old, I'm going to find homes for them."

"Do you come here every day?"

Megan nodded.

"You remind me of my daughter," the driver said. "When she was your age, she was always feeding some stray cat, or trying to save a baby bird that fell out of its nest, or begging me to pick up a lost dog that was running alongside a busy street."

"Would your daughter like to have one of the kittens when they're ready for adoption?" Megan asked.

The cell phone in his pocket rang. He took out the phone, pushed a button, and said, "This is Dale. Oh. Can you verify that I'm supposed to clear the land today for that apartment building on the corner of 148th, by the freeway? There's a kid here who claims the project's been put on hold until some wild cats get moved out of the field." He covered the phone and said to Megan, "She can't reach Mr. Colby. She's going to ask someone else."

Megan's nervousness returned. What if Mr. Colby had not told anyone else about the cats? What if the woman in the office came back and told the driver to proceed with bulldozing the field? What would Megan do then?

A minute later the driver spoke into the receiver again. "Okay," he said. "Thanks for checking."

He closed the cell phone and put it back in his pocket.

Megan held her breath.

"Nobody in the office knows anything about the cats," he said. "Most of the staff left early today because of the balloon festival. Colby Construction sponsors one of the balloons, and this year they're also selling doughnuts and hot cider, to raise money for the new library."

Megan pressed her lips together, trying to keep back the tears. "Will you wait until you reach Mr. Colby?" she asked. "Please?"

"I'll tell you what," the driver said. "I was late getting here today and now it's after four o'clock. Since I can't finish the job this afternoon anyway, I won't start it until tomorrow morning."

"Thank you," Megan said. "Will you keep trying to call Mr. Colby?"

"The only number I have is the office; they close at five. But they said he checks his messages. Maybe he'll call me tonight."

"What if he doesn't?" Megan asked.

"Then I won't have any choice but to go ahead and clear the land tomorrow. I don't usually work on Saturday, but this is a rush order that was supposed to be finished today. I said I'd do the job, and I'm obligated to do it. As it is, I'm a day behind their schedule."

"What time will you be here in the morning?" she asked.

"I usually start at seven-thirty."

"I'm going to the balloon festival," Megan said. "I'll look for Mr. Colby at the booth selling doughnuts and cider."

But what if she didn't find him? Thousands of people attended the festival every year, and just because his company was sponsoring a food booth didn't mean he would be working there.

"Good luck," the driver said.

"Thanks." She turned and walked toward her bike.

I'll need plenty of luck, Megan thought. If Mr. Colby's own office can't get hold of him, what chance do I have?

All she could do was try. She would look for him at the balloon festival, and if she didn't find him there, she would call the number he had given her.

She remembered that Mr. Colby had crossed off the number on the business card and written in a different number. Maybe he had given her his home number — or maybe Mom had it, because of the book club. She hoped so. She would try to call him, and keep trying, until she got an answer.

If she had not spoken to Brice Colby by seven tomorrow morning, she would call the TV hot-line number, and the newspapers, and all her friends. She would ask people to picket, with signs. If she had to, she would stand in front of the bulldozer and prevent the driver from moving it forward.

Megan reached her bike and mounted it. As she rode away from the field, she glanced back at the big yellow bulldozer.

On second thought, she wasn't sure she would have the courage to stand in front of that machine if it was headed toward her.

She hoped she would not have to find out.

12

It was past four-thirty when Megan got home. Mrs. Perk and Kylie were eating grilled cheese sandwiches and tomato soup.

"I was getting worried," Mrs. Perk said.

"There was a bulldozer at the field. The driver was starting to clear the land when I got there."

"I'll call Brice while you eat your dinner," Mrs. Perk said. "If he isn't home, I'll explain the problem to Ruthann."

Megan washed her hands, transferred her sandwich from the pan to her plate, and warmed her cup of soup in the microwave.

"You have to eat all your dinner if you want cotton candy," Kylie told her.

Mrs. Perk looked up the phone number, dialed, waited, and then hung up. "I got their answering machine," she said. "There's no use leaving a message, since we won't be here tonight. If he called back, he'd just get our machine. I'll try again when we get home."

"Is that bulldozer going to squash

Dinkle?" Kylie asked, her lips trembling.

"Dinkle isn't in the field," Mrs. Perk said. "Dinkle is safe at home with Mr. Leefton."

"Not Dinkle the dog," Kylie said.

"She means one of the kittens," Megan explained. "The one she wants to keep."

Kylie nodded. "I named my kitten Dinkle," she said. "He's going to purr when I pet him."

"Your kitten will not get squashed," Megan said. "I promise."

She hoped she could keep that promise.

As they drove to the balloon festival, questions filled Megan's mind. Why had Mr. Colby made such a point of telling her that the building permit was being delayed for a month, if no permit was required in order to clear the land?

Why had Mr. Colby said he would find out who owned the property? If his company was building the apartments, surely he already knew the property owner. Maybe he even owned it himself. Was Mr. Colby only pretending to help her?

The bulldozer driver had said it was a rush job — why? If it was so important to clear the field quickly, why didn't the people in the office at Colby Construction know about it?

Maybe it's just a mix-up, Megan thought. Maybe some other building site is a rush job and whoever hired the bulldozer made a mistake and gave the wrong address.

A new question arose: What if the threatening note was not from the driver of the tan car? What if it had nothing at all to do with the accident?

Megan did not need to look at the red words in order to remember them. *If you want the cats to live, don't tell anyone.* Until now she had assumed the note meant: don't tell anyone who was driving the tan car.

What if the note meant: don't tell anyone about the cats? The note made just as much sense that way. Why would anyone want to keep the cats secret?

The only people who knew Megan was feeding the cats were Mom, Kylie, Mr. Colby, and Officer Rupp. None of them wanted the field cleared, nor would they have left a menacing note.

Maybe Mr. Colby had told other people about the cats and the note was from one of them. Perhaps someone she didn't even know wanted Megan to keep quiet about the cats until it was too late to save them. If so, had that person arranged for the field to be cleared as soon as possible?

She could not imagine what anyone would stand to gain from destroying the feral cats. Yet someone had left the anonymous message, and someone had ordered the bulldozer to clear the field. The question was who? And why?

Megan's head ached from trying to figure it out. She was determined to speak to Mr. Colby as soon as possible.

Mrs. Perk gave two dollars to the parking attendant and found a spot in the airport parking lot.

Megan pushed her concerns aside as they walked toward the colorful hot-air balloons.

"Let's buy our cotton candy first," Kylie said.

"We came to see the balloons," Mrs. Perk said.

Rows of balloons, each tethered to the ground with a rope, filled the airport's three runways. A thick wicker basket large enough to hold six to eight people rested on the ground beneath each balloon. Cords spaced about a foot apart around the bottom edge of the balloons were attached to the rims of the baskets.

A heavy metal frame went up from each corner of the square baskets, bending inward just beneath the center of the balloon's opening. Gas jets rested in the middle of the frame.

Megan, Mrs. Perk, and Kylie walked toward the first balloon in the row. The narrow open end, toward the basket, was dark pink; the fat part of the balloon was light pink.

"It looks like a giant cotton candy," Kylie said.

The next balloon was purple and gold. Large letters around the center of the balloon spelled out the name of a computer store.

One balloon was silver, dotted with blue stars. Another looked like a checkerboard with every square a different color: red, orange, yellow, green, blue, and even black.

Each balloon was about thirty feet high and eighteen feet around at the largest point.

Four balloons in the first row rose upward. Each pilot released just enough gas to lift the balloon fifty feet into the air.

The balloons hovered over the airfield for five minutes and then descended.

"Wouldn't it be fun to ride in one?" Megan said.

"Fun but expensive," Mrs. Perk replied. "The sunset rides from Balloon Adventures are seventy-five dollars per person."

"Yikes," Megan said.

"Cotton candy is only one dollar," Kylie said. "A real bargain."

"I give up," Mrs. Perk said. "Where do we get it?"

Kylie pointed eagerly to a line of food

booths along one side of the airport terminal. As they started toward the booths, Megan spotted Mr. Colby, partway across the festival grounds.

"There's Mr. Colby," she said. "Let's go talk to him."

"Where?" Mrs. Perk asked.

Megan pointed across the balloon exhibit to the next runway.

Mrs. Perk looked where Megan was pointing. "I don't see him," she said.

"Over there. He's in the basket of that green-and-blue striped balloon. Come on."

"That's the wrong way!" Kylie protested. "You said we could get cotton candy now!"

"I'll go with Kylie to buy her treat," Mrs. Perk said. "If I don't find you and Brice, I'll meet you back here, by this checkered balloon."

Megan made her way between two balloons to the next runway. When she reached the green-and-blue striped balloon, she saw that a large sign on the basket said COLBY CONSTRUCTION COMPANY. Mr. Colby was in the basket, releasing just enough gas to keep the balloon fully inflated.

"Hi, Mr. Colby," Megan said.

He did not look at her.

Megan tapped him on the arm.

"Hello!" she said.

He seemed surprised to see her. "Oh, it's you," he said.

"I'm so glad I found you," Megan said. "There's been a terrible mix-up. On my way home from school, I went to the field where the cats live, and a bulldozer was beginning to clear away all the grass. If I hadn't stopped the driver, the whole field would have been cleared."

Mr. Colby's face flushed with anger. "You stopped him?"

"Yes."

"How much did he get done?"

"He didn't do any of it," Megan said. "He quit when I told him about the cats. He tried to call you, but you had already left the office and you didn't answer your pager."

"You told the driver about the cats?"

"Yes. But he said he'd been instructed to clear that field, and he's going to start again at seven-thirty tomorrow morning unless he hears from you before then. His name is Dale Burrows."

A muscle in Mr. Colby's cheek twitched; he clenched his fists.

"This could have been a disaster," Megan said. "What if I hadn't gone to the field today? Or what if he had started earlier, while I was still in school?"

The friendly smile that the man had always worn when he sat in his blue truck did not appear. Instead he looked furious. Megan assumed he was angry because the field had almost been cleared without his knowledge.

"I'm so glad I found you," Megan said. "I was going to call the television stations and the animal-welfare agencies, but it will be much easier for you to stop the clearing than for me to do it."

He stared at her for a second.

"How would you like to ride in my hot-air balloon?"

The question was so unexpected that it took a moment for it to sink in. When it did, Megan said, "I'd love it!"

"Get in the basket."

"You mean, now? You're going to give me a ride tonight?"

"This row of balloons is scheduled to go up next. If you want to ride with me, climb in."

Megan hesitated. "I probably should ask my mom if it's okay," she said.

"There isn't time. I just tested the wind, and it's perfect. If you want a ride, it's now or never."

Megan was sure Mom would say yes. After all, she knew Mr. Colby, and she had said he was a dependable person. The balloons didn't go far during these demonstrations; Megan would be back on the ground in only a few minutes. When would she ever get another chance like this?

Megan put her hands on the rim of the basket and climbed inside.

Mr. Colby untied the rope that tethered the balloon.

He opened a valve. *Whoosh!* Megan heard the gas leave the jets and enter the inside of the balloon.

He tossed a large bag of sand out of the basket. The balloon rose slowly.

Megan stood at the edge of the basket, looking toward the row of food booths. Wouldn't it be great if Mom and Kylie saw her up here? Maybe she could spot them down below and wave to them.

More gas whooshed into the balloon.

They were above the other balloons now. It was like looking down on a brightly colored fairyland.

"Hey!" someone yelled. "What are you doing?"

Megan looked toward the voice. The call came from a man who stood where the Colby Construction balloon had been tethered. He was looking up toward her and waving.

"Hey!" he shouted again. "You can't take

a passenger up now. Bring her down!"

"That man is yelling at you," Megan said. "He says we should go down."

"He's not my boss," Mr. Colby muttered. "Not anymore."

Whoosh. Whoosh. More gas entered the cavity; the balloon went higher.

Megan clung to the side of the basket.

"Shane!" the man on the ground shouted. "Come back right now, or you're fired!"

Shane? A quiver of apprehension ran down the back of Megan's neck. Why was the man calling Mr. Colby by the name Shane, when his name was Brice?

Megan saw that the other balloons in their row were still tethered. Two more people now stood where the Colby balloon had been; they pointed upward. One turned and ran toward the airport terminal.

Whoosh. The balloon continued to rise. The balloons Megan had viewed earlier had not gone nearly this high during their demonstrations, and several had risen at the same time. The Colby Construction balloon was the only one in the air.

When the balloon got higher, it drifted east, toward Desolation Hill. Megan watched as they moved farther from the airport.

Soon the crowds of people at the balloon festival looked like small action figures.

Even the giant balloons seemed like bright polka dots on a large quilt.

This is wrong, Megan thought. We should not be going so far from the festival.

"Don't you think we should go down now?" she said. "We're a long way from the airport."

"We'll go down," he replied, "but not at the airport."

13

Megan watched the man. Was he Brice Colby, or was he someone named Shane?

He consulted a sheet of paper, looked at his watch again, then let more gas out of the jets.

"What are you doing?" she asked.

"We're going on a little trip," the man said.

A trip! In the dark? Megan wanted to shout. Are you out of your mind? You can't fly a hot-air balloon at night. They don't have lights or radar like airplanes have. You'll crash!

Fearing that he was, indeed, out of his mind, she struggled to keep her voice calm. "Where are you going?" she asked. "Why are you taking me along?"

He did not look at her when he replied, but his voice was sharp with rage. "You were warned not to tell anyone about those cats," he said.

Megan tried not to panic. "Warned?" she said. "What do you mean?"

"If you had done what I told you and kept quiet about the cats, I wouldn't have to take you with me."

"Did *you* leave that note?" Megan asked.

"My plan was working perfectly until you came along. I don't intend to let some kid and a bunch of wild cats foul up my life."

"What plan?" she said. "Where are you taking me?"

He ignored the questions and released more gas from the jets. The bright balloons at the airport were now only a glow in the distance. The last pink light of the sunset faded to darkness. How could he see where the balloon was going?

"You aren't Brice Colby are you?" Megan asked.

"I never said I was."

"You gave me his business card when you told me to call you."

He shrugged, as if to say, so what?

She could see the top of Desolation Hill, a faint outline against the shadowy horizon. The balloon was headed directly toward the peak.

"Who are you?" Megan asked.

Instead of answering, he adjusted the gas again.

"Your name is Shane, isn't it?" Megan said.

"Shut up. I need to fly this balloon."

Fly it where? Megan wondered. Dozens of other questions crowded into her mind, but she didn't ask them. She was afraid if she distracted him too much, the balloon would crash into Desolation Hill.

It was totally quiet up high. Except for the occasional *whoosh* of gas leaving the jets, Megan was surrounded by silence. If I can't hear people, she thought, they can't hear me. Even if I scream, no one will know.

Darkness enveloped the balloon; Megan saw nothing now in any direction. She felt as if she had left the Earth behind and was drifting in a black universe.

The only light was the balloon itself, glowing blue and green against the night sky.

The man, Shane, seemed unconcerned. He acted as if he had flown this route before in total darkness and knew from his written notes exactly how much gas the balloon needed.

He's the one who ordered the field to be cleared, Megan realized. He pretended to help me so I wouldn't get Feline Friends involved in the cat rescue until it was too late. He left the threatening note, too, although she couldn't figure out his motive. Now he was taking her with him on some wild scheme in order to keep her from stopping the bulldozer tomorrow morning.

She watched him carefully. Every few minutes, he put one hand on his jacket pocket, as if checking to be sure that whatever he had inside was still there. The movement seemed spontaneous, a gesture he made without thinking about it.

She saw a cellular phone in the bottom of the basket. I can call for help, she thought, and then realized that no one could help her. Not until she was safely back on the ground.

Something brushed the bottom of the basket. Megan gasped.

Shane released more gas. The balloon rose a few feet.

Megan looked over the edge of the basket and saw leafy branches. The balloon was skimming along, just above some treetops. We must be going over the hill, she thought. The balloon had continued to drift away from town as it rose; these trees must be on the top of Desolation Hill.

She could not guess their final destination. Desolation Hill was the first in a series of foothills leading toward the Cascade Mountains. Dense forests covered the hills. Why would he fly into such a wilderness? If they crashed now, they might never be found.

A few minutes later Shane turned the gas jets down. The balloon began to sink. Gradually he let less and less gas into the opening, and the balloon descended. The hill now cut off the wind that had pushed them eastward, so the balloon dropped without drifting.

He's going to land, Megan realized. What if they ran into power lines or crashed into some big trees? What if she was thrown out? She wondered how high up the balloon was.

It was completely dark below them — no town, no lights from a highway. She gripped the edge of the basket and hoped they came down in a clearing.

What will happen next? Megan wondered. He had said he had a plan, but what about me? If we land safely, then what?

"Sit down," he said.

Megan sat.

Shane crouched beside her. Sweat trickled down the sides of his face, and his breathing was rapid. He's nervous, Megan realized, and her own throat felt tight with fear.

Shane turned the gas off. The flame flickered out. With the gas off, darkness filled the basket.

"We may bump when we touch down," he said. "Hang on."

A short time later, the basket banged against the ground, bounced upward, hit again, and finally tipped over on one side.

Megan managed to hang on to the edge and not be thrown out. The basket slid a few feet on its side before it came to a stop.

The balloon slowly deflated, coming to rest on the ground.

Megan crawled out of the basket and stood up. She wanted to run away, but she had no idea where she was or which way to go. She smelled cedar trees but could not see them in the dark.

Shane got out of the basket, too. He walked away from her as if he knew exactly where he was going.

The cell phone, Megan thought. Here's my chance to get the telephone and call for help. Even though I don't know where we are, I can say we've landed. The other pilots at the festival would be able to figure out approximately how far a balloon could go in the amount of time they had been gone.

She crawled back into the basket, feeling in the darkness for the telephone. She found it, but it was too dark to see the numbers. Holding the phone, she got out of the basket.

Suddenly bright lights shone directly at her. Megan put her hand up to her eyes to shield them from the glare. When she squinted toward the lights, she saw that they were headlights. He had a car waiting here, she realized. He must have brought the balloon down exactly where he intended to land.

Quickly she opened the cell phone, hit 9-1-1, and then pushed "Send." The lighted message said, "No Service."

Disappointment sent tears to her eyes. She was too far out in the wilderness; the cellular phone could not help her. She closed the phone and looked back at Shane.

He had removed his jacket. He opened the trunk, took something out, and ran toward the balloon.

Megan saw that he carried a large red plastic container. It said GASOLINE on the side.

Shane began pouring gasoline on the basket.

Horrified, Megan backed away. Shane's plan seemed chillingly clear. He wanted it to seem as if the balloon had crashed. Before he drove away, he intended to set the balloon on fire!

They were miles from any fire station. They were miles from any people. The fire would probably never be spotted. By the time the balloon was found, if it was ever found, there would be nothing left but ashes.

Shane circled the basket, dribbling gasoline on it. Then he walked along the edge of the balloon, pouring gasoline on the blue-and-green fabric.

As she watched him, Megan moved slowly toward the car. She wanted to get beyond the lights, so he couldn't see her.

Intent on what he was doing, Shane didn't pay any attention to Megan. He stopped twice to wipe the sweat from his face with a bandana, then continued to pour gasoline on the balloon.

Megan made it to the car. She looked in the window and saw Shane's jacket on the seat. She wondered what was in the pocket that he had kept touching. Whatever it was, it must be important to him. Perhaps she should take it, in case she needed to bargain with him.

She pushed the button on the handle of the car door, relieved that it was not locked. She eased the door open.

Keeping her eyes on Shane, she put the telephone on the seat while she reached for the jacket, unzipped the pocket, and removed a thick envelope.

Shane shook the container, as if it were empty, and turned back toward the car.

Instantly Megan pushed the door shut and crouched down beside the car. She put the envelope in the pocket of her windbreaker.

Megan feared he would see her; she dropped to her stomach and slithered under the vehicle. Her heart thumped wildly. What if he drove off now, with her under the car? She flattened herself on the ground.

She heard the trunk slam shut. She saw his shoes move along the side of the car toward the driver's door. He paused, as if looking in the window, and then walked back toward the balloon.

His hands were empty now; he had put the gasoline container in the trunk.

Megan slid out from under the car and peeked over the top. She saw him disconnect one of the cords that ran from the balloon to the basket. He held it out, as if judging its length.

Holding the end of the cord, he looked at the basket. Then he turned his head, looking all around.

"Hey!" he said. "Where are you?" He seemed to realize for the first time that Megan was not beside the balloon where he had last seen her.

He gripped the cord in his fist as he looked for her.

Understanding hit Megan as if she'd been punched in the stomach. He plans to use that cord to tie me to the basket, she thought. Then he'll set the basket on fire!

14

Megan dropped to her hands and knees, and crawled away from the car, hoping that the vehicle would shield her from his sight.

The thick underbrush scratched her face; her palms came down on pebbles and thorny branches.

There must be a road, Megan thought. He drove the car here. It was a plain sedan, not an all-terrain vehicle. If I can hide from him until he leaves, I can follow the road and get help.

"Hey, kid!" he called. "It's time to go back. Come and get in the basket."

Did he think she was completely stupid? Megan kept crawling, ignoring the brambles that slashed at her cheeks.

She reached a tree, and then another; she was moving beyond the clearing. Good. Megan crawled behind a big tree and then stood up. Looking back around the tree, she saw Shane run to the car.

He knows I'm hiding from him, Megan

thought. She held her breath, wondering if he would bother to search for her or if he would get in the car and drive off.

He looked inside the car, then got down on one knee and looked underneath it. Megan was glad she had crawled away from the car.

He circled the car slowly, as if unable to believe that she was not there in plain sight.

He returned to the balloon and ran around it. He kicked the basket in frustration.

"You come here!" he shouted. "If you don't, I'll leave you to starve to death in the forest. You'll get eaten by a grizzly bear."

Megan stayed still.

The man's voice rose to a shriek, as if his anger was completely out of control. "So you like cats?" he yelled. He shook both fists in the air. "Wait until a mountain lion sinks his jaws into you. Then see how much you like cats!"

Megan shuddered.

He took something out of his pants pocket and flicked one hand against the other. Megan realized he was striking a match.

He flung the lighted match onto the balloon fabric. A path of fire raced along the edge of the balloon, following the trail of gasoline.

Shane lit another match and threw it in the wicker basket.

Poof! Flames erupted, filling the center of the basket.

Shane did not wait to watch the balloon burn. He ran to the car and got in.

Boom! The propane tank in the basket exploded. Pieces of the metal frame that had held the gas jets flew into the forest. Flaming wicker shot into the air like rockets.

Megan ducked, holding her hands over her head.

Shane started the engine.

I need to be a better witness than I was last time, Megan thought. She wasn't worried about describing the man; she knew exactly what he looked like. But if she got out of this alive, the police would ask her about the car as well.

While Shane made a U-turn, Megan looked at the license plate. There was just enough firelight for her to see it: KKB 513. She repeated it to herself: KKB 513.

With no way to write it down, she feared she would forget it, so she made up words to go with the letters. *Kittens. Kylie. Balloon.*

There were five cats. Thirteen was considered an unlucky number, and this was definitely Megan's unlucky day. *Kittens, Kylie, balloon;* five cats and unlucky thirteen.

Shane drove away from the fire.

From her place behind the tree, Megan watched the car bump along. The road was little more than a path, but she could tell it led down the hill. She watched until the red taillights disappeared into the trees.

By then the entire balloon was on fire. Yellow and red flames leaped skyward, illuminating the meadow where the balloon had dropped. Shane had landed close to the eastern edge of the grassy area; if the balloon had traveled much farther, they would have come down in the woods.

Some tall grass next to the blazing basket started to burn. The fire spread away from the basket, as more grass and underbrush ignited.

This could start a forest fire, Megan thought. This whole hill could go up in flames!

She ran to the burning grass and stamped on it, smothering the flames with her shoes.

A patch of weeds near the top end of the balloon caught fire. Megan tried to stamp it out, too, but those flames were higher. They leaped around her ankles, scorching the cuffs of her jeans.

Megan jumped aside. She took off her windbreaker and raised it over her head to beat at the fire.

She remembered the envelope. Whatever was in it, Shane had acted as if it were important. She took the envelope out of her windbreaker and wedged it into the back pocket of her jeans before she flung the windbreaker down on the fire.

Whack! Whack! She hit the flames over and over until only smoke remained.

Sparks rained down. A clump of weeds flared up. Megan circled the balloon, stamping out hot spots that threatened to spread.

Maybe someone will see the fire, she thought. Maybe the Forest Service has a lookout tower that has a view of this area. Perhaps an airplane will fly over and the fire will be visible from the air. By now, people at the balloon festival would have notified the police; maybe a police helicopter was already searching for her.

The fire died down within minutes. The balloon was completely gone; only a charred, smoking section of the meadow remained where the beautiful blue-and-green fabric had landed. The basket continued to smolder.

Megan wondered if she should keep the fire going. She could break branches from the trees and feed the flames. She could stay near the fire so that if a helicopter did fly over, the pilot would be sure to see her.

But what if no air search was in progress, or they didn't fly over this area?

I should hike down the path that Shane drove, she decided. It must connect with a road at the bottom of the hill. If there are grizzly bears and mountain lions in these woods, the sooner I get out of here, the better.

The path down the hill was hard to follow in the dark. Megan tried to stay in one of the two lines where Shane's tires had flattened the grass.

Smoke from the burned balloon stung her nostrils. Acrid with gasoline, it hung in the air. She hoped any grizzly bears or mountain lions would smell it, too, and stay away from this part of the forest.

As she walked she listened for sounds in the woods around her. She heard only leaves rustling and a far-off hoot owl.

A half-moon rose high enough to send a faint light through the woods. Megan walked faster.

Light beamed through the distant trees; then Megan heard a motor. Someone was coming! Headlights flashed on the path below her.

They've found me, Megan thought, but her gladness lasted only a second. It seemed too soon. Even if the fire had been spotted, a rescue car could not have discovered this little-used path so quickly.

She stopped. What if it was Shane, coming back?

Megan left the path and pushed through the underbrush. She passed a clump of trees and kept going.

She came to a large fir tree and hid behind it.

The car chugged closer, climbing the path. If it was a different car, she would rush out and call to the driver. If it was Shane, she would remain behind the fir tree and hope he couldn't see her.

The headlights came around a bend a short distance from where Megan had left the path. She pressed herself against the rough bark. The tree smelled like Christmastime; Megan blinked back tears as she thought of Mom and Kylie.

When the car passed her, she looked out and recognized Shane's white Ford.

She stayed behind the tree after the car passed. The lights faded from her sight, but in only a few minutes she heard Shane shout, "It's mine! What have you done with it?"

She realized he had come back to get the envelope. Curious, Megan removed the envelope from her pocket and tore it open. She tipped the contents toward the moonlight.

"Oh!" she whispered. No wonder he was so upset; the envelope that she had taken was full of money. *Lots* of money!

As Megan put the envelope back in her pocket, she wondered who the money belonged to. Probably not Shane, she thought. If it was rightfully his, he would not have to stage a fake balloon accident and sneak away in the night.

She heard him yell, "You won't get away with this. I'll find you! I'll track you down! And when I do . . ." His voice trailed away, as if he could not think of any punishment terrible enough.

Soon the headlights appeared again, going back down the hill. Megan crouched in the dirt behind the big tree. The car moved slowly; she knew he was searching for her as he drove.

He had the window down now. Even though he did not see her, he continued to yell at her as he drove. "I'll get you! I'll get you!" He sounded wild and out of control, as if his rage had overcome his brain.

The headlights zigzagged on the path. Megan wasn't sure if he drove that way on purpose, trying to watch for her on both sides, or if he was so distraught that he couldn't control the car.

Would he be able to tell that the under-brush was bent down where she had left the path? Would he stop and follow the broken brush to where she was hiding?

If he did, should she hide the envelope and pretend she had never seen it? Or should she give it to him as a way to squelch his anger?

15

Megan decided to hide the money. Giving it back to him would be proof that she had taken it in the first place; that might make him even angrier.

She dug into the dirt with her fingers, making a flat trench about six inches wide. She laid the envelope in the shallow hole, then shoved the loose dirt on top of it. Unless a person knew exactly where to look, the envelope would never be noticed.

As the car drove closer, he screamed, "Your cats will be dead tomorrow morning, and you'll be next!"

The front of the car angled toward the other side of the path as it approached her. Megan held her breath, hoping he would keep it aimed that way. Just as the car reached her, it swerved back toward her side, and for an instant the lights pointed straight at the tree she was behind.

But the car slowly passed her. Then the brake lights came on.

The car backed up. It stopped when the lights reached the place where Megan had left the path.

Megan held her breath. She heard the car door open. She heard him crash toward her through the bushes.

I'll have to run for it, she thought. If I stay where I am, he'll find me for sure.

She stood up, staying behind the tree. She heard him charging closer. The woods were thick behind her; there was no point trying to run that way.

Her only hope was to somehow get past him and run back to the car. If she could make it to the car and get inside, she could lock him out. Maybe she could even drive the car away.

"I know you're here!" he shouted. "I can see where you walked."

In a moment, Megan knew, he would come around the side of the tree. There was no way to be certain which side of the tree he would appear on.

She had gone to her left as she approached the clump of trees. Since he seemed to be following her trail, she hoped he would go to his left, too. She prepared to run around the other side.

He would be only a foot or two away when he saw her. Could she possibly get by him before he grabbed her?

The headlights shining behind him caused his shadow to precede him as he approached the tree. Megan saw it coming, first the head, then the body. He was almost there.

She waited until all of the shadow was visible.

Just as Shane stepped around the side of the tree, she slipped around the other side and took off.

"What the . . . ?" He stopped, momentarily stunned by her unexpected appearance so nearby.

He recovered quickly and ran after her.

Megan raced through the underbrush, fearing she would trip and fall but not daring to go slowly.

Behind her, Shane shouted, "I've got you now, you little thief! You'll never get away!"

Megan dashed toward the car. She saw that he had left the driver's door open. She ran to it, got in, and slammed the door shut, quickly locking it behind her. She leaned across the seat and locked the door on the passenger's side. The back doors, thank goodness, were already locked.

Shane reached the car and began pounding on the door. He pressed his face against the window and yelled at Megan. He began to kick the door, over and over.

His face contorted with anger. He hardly looked like the same man Megan had talked to about rescuing the cats.

He picked up a rock the size of a softball and bashed it against the window next to Megan.

He's going to break the window, Megan thought. The glass will shatter, and he'll reach through the opening and unlock the door.

The keys dangled in the ignition.

Megan had never driven a car. She had watched Mom drive, but Megan's only experience behind a steering wheel was in the bumper cars at the county fair.

I have to try, she told herself. I can't just sit here and let him smash the window and get to me.

Bang! Bang! He continued to hit the side window with the rock.

Megan turned the key. The engine sputtered and then stopped. She turned the key again. This time, the engine started.

At the sound of the engine, Shane pounded faster on the window. A crack appeared, and then another, and another. The window looked like a spiderweb, but it stayed in place.

Gas, Megan thought. I have to put my foot on the gas pedal. She pushed her right foot down on a floor pedal. The engine roared but the car stayed where it was.

Megan saw a short handle sticking out from the steering wheel. She thought she needed to move it to shift the car so it would drive.

She pulled down on the handle. The car rolled forward.

Shane ran alongside it, slamming the rock against the window.

Megan pushed on the gas pedal again. The car lurched ahead, went off the left side of the path, and ran over three small huckleberry bushes.

Shane jumped away from the car.

Megan yanked the steering wheel to the right. The car zoomed back across the path and off the other side, narrowly missing a tree. She turned the wheel slightly left, angling the car back to the path. Driving isn't as easy as it looks, Megan thought.

Shane ran after her as soon as she was back on the path, but the path was too narrow for him to stay alongside.

Megan couldn't go fast for fear of leaving the path and crashing, but she gradually pulled away from Shane.

Thunk! Megan jumped at the noise, thinking she had run into something she hadn't seen.

Thunk! Thunk! Shane was throwing rocks at the car. The rocks hit the back window and the trunk. One flew completely over the car and landed on the hood.

It was hard to concentrate on steering the car when large rocks kept banging against it. She looked in the rearview mirror to see how far back Shane was. Just then the path curved to the right. Megan didn't turn the wheel soon enough; the left front fender grazed an alder tree.

A branch knocked against the window next to Megan. The cracked window broke. Pieces of glass flew inward, gashing Megan's face and neck.

She winced at the pain but kept her hands on the steering wheel as chunks of glass landed in her lap. She got the car back in the tracks.

Rocks hit the rear of the car less often; she was getting farther ahead of him. Picking up rocks to throw slows him down, she thought. You would think he could figure that out.

For the first time, she glanced at the speedometer; she was driving less than ten miles per hour, but on the bumpy hard-to-see path it felt as if she were speeding.

She came to a straight stretch of path and pushed the gas pedal down farther. After that, no more rocks hit the car.

The path seemed to go on forever. It must come out at a road eventually. Megan thought. It has to! But when? How long would it take?

Her eyes ached from staring so intently at the path. Her fingers were stiff from holding the wheel so hard, and her face hurt where the glass had cut her.

She longed to stop the car and examine her wounds, but she couldn't take a chance that he would catch up. If he got there now, with the window broken, she had no way to keep him out.

16

Ten minutes after Megan started down the hill in the car, she bumped across a shallow ditch and on to a paved road. She turned right, pulled to the edge of the road and put her foot on the brake pedal. The car jerked to a stop.

She switched on the overhead light and looked at her face in the rearview mirror. The cuts hurt but none seemed deep enough to require stitches. She knew she was lucky that no glass had hit her eyes.

She looked around for some kind of landmark so that she could direct the police to the path up the hill. She saw only woods on both sides of the road.

I'll have to leave a marker on the side of the road, she thought. Otherwise they'll never find the path — or Shane, or the envelope full of money.

She put the car in park, turned off the engine, and took the key out of the ignition. She got out of the car, opened the trunk, and removed the empty red gasoline container. She set it on the side of the road where it would be clearly visible to anyone driving down the road.

When she got back in the car, she saw the telephone on the seat. This road is more open than the forest was, Megan thought. Maybe the cellular signal can get through from here.

Once again she pushed 9-1-1, and this time the lighted panel showed the numbers she had dialed. She pushed "Send."

Her call was answered instantly.

"My name is Megan Perk, and I was in the hot-air balloon that left the festival."

"Are you all right?"

"Yes."

"Where are you now?"

"I don't know. The balloon landed in a clearing just on the other side of Desolation Hill. I followed a path down the hill, and I'm on a road but there aren't any cars."

"Every police officer in the county is looking for you. Are you alone?"

"Yes, but I'm in a car."

"Where is Shane Turner?"

"I got away from Shane and drove his car down the hill."

"By yourself?" The voice sounded incredulous.

"Yes."

"Can you describe the car?"

Megan felt a small surge of pride as she replied, "It's a white Ford sedan. License number: K as in *kitten*, K as in —" She started to say *Kylie* but instead said *kitten* again. "B as in *balloon*, five thirteen."

"Stay where you are. We'll find you." Static crackled on the line. The voice faded briefly, then came back. "Megan, are you still there?"

"I'm afraid to wait where I am," Megan said. "I don't know how far behind me Shane is, and he's really angry. He threatened to kill me."

"Lock the car doors. Stay inside."

"He broke the window. I'm going to keep driving."

"The sheriff is on his way. So is the highway patrol." The voice faded again, and then the line went dead. The lighted panel on the phone turned dark.

The battery is probably run down, Megan thought. It didn't matter. She had told the dispatcher as much as she could about her location.

She was too nervous to wait where she was. Shane might not be too far behind. She had driven slowly, and now she had used several minutes talking to the emergency dispatcher. Shane could come out of the woods on to the road at any time.

She started the engine and drove away. It was easier to drive now that she was on a regular road, so she pushed on the gas pedal until the speedometer said twenty miles per hour.

Shane would never catch her now. Relief eased the tension from her aching muscles.

She was certain that the gasoline container would lead the authorities to the path, but she wondered if she would ever be able to find the envelope full of cash. She realized she had not even mentioned the money to the dispatcher.

I have a whole lot to tell the police, Megan thought. I need to tell them about the money, and that Shane burned the balloon, and how to find the path where Shane is. I need to show them the note he left me about the cats.

A distant siren broke into Megan's thoughts. They've found the right road, she thought.

Megan looked ahead but saw no lights coming toward her. The siren got louder. And louder.

Finally Megan realized that the sound came from behind her. She slowed the car, looked over her shoulder, and saw headlights. Headlights *and* flashing red lights!

Megan slammed on the brake, not caring if the car jerked or not.

Seconds later, two highway patrol cars stopped beside her. The officers rushed toward her as Megan got out.

"Are you okay?" one officer asked.

"Yes," Megan said, although now that the danger was over, her legs shook. She leaned against the car.

"Your mother is going to be one relieved woman," the officer said. "She's been frantic!" He radioed the information that Megan was safe.

Megan sat in the squad car and told the officers everything that had happened. Two more police cars arrived. They stayed long enough to hear about the path and the red gasoline container near it; then they took off in search of Shane.

"We set up a temporary headquarters at the airport," one officer told her. "Your mother is waiting for you there."

As he turned the car around, Megan realized she had been driving in the wrong direction.

During the ride, the police continued to question Megan. They were astonished when she told them about the envelope full of thousand-dollar bills.

When the squad car pulled into the airport, Mrs. Perk and Kylie ran out of the terminal to greet Megan. They were followed by a paramedic, and a man and woman Megan didn't know. She recognized him as the man who had yelled at Shane as the balloon took off.

Mrs. Perk hugged Megan. "Are you all right?" she asked.

"I'm fine," Megan said.

Her mother had the medic examine her anyway.

He checked Megan thoroughly and treated the cuts on her face. When he left, Mrs. Perk introduced the couple with her as Brice and Ruthann Colby.

"Shane burned up your balloon," Megan said.

"What?" Mr. Colby said.

"He wanted you to think it crashed."

"Oh no!" Mrs. Colby said.

"I should not have hired him," Mr. Colby said. "I knew he'd be trouble."

"It's my fault," Mrs. Colby said. She began to cry. "I thought the anger-management class and the counseling he got in prison had helped. I thought he had changed."

"He changed all right," Mr. Colby said, his face red with anger. "He added kidnapping and arson to his list of crimes."

"I'm so ashamed of my brother," Mrs. Colby said. "I never dreamed he would harm a child."

"He's mentally unbalanced," Mr. Colby said. "He gets so angry that he goes completely out of his head."

The police interrupted, to tell them Shane had been caught.

"What will he be charged with this time?" Mr. Colby asked.

"Abduction of a minor. Probably arson. Maybe theft — we've had no big robbery reported, but Megan says Shane had a large amount of cash in his pocket, and he was carrying identification for a William Bradburn."

"How much cash?" Mr. Colby said.

"Almost twenty thousand dollars."

Mrs. Colby gasped. "Where would Shane get that much money?"

"Not from any legal source," Mr. Colby said.

"It might be a good idea to audit your company's accounts," the officer suggested.

"I'll do that," Mr. Colby said. "I'll take a look yet tonight."

17

"I thought that bad man was going to hurt you," Kylie said. "I was so scared that I couldn't even sing."

"I was scared, too," Megan admitted.

"He was a dirty rotten rat," Kylie declared. "He deserves to go to jail."

Megan agreed.

"I'm glad you're okay," Kylie said. "I would be lonesome without you."

Megan hugged her sister. In spite of Kylie's endless songs and chatter, she knew she would be lonely without Kylie, too.

Mrs. Perk said, "I told the Colbys about the cats, and about how Shane pretended to be Brice."

Mr. Colby said, "I called Dale Burrows and told him not to clear the field."

"I'm a member of Feline Friends," Mrs. Colby said. "We have what we call a TNR program for feral cats: trap, neuter, and release. We use humane traps to catch them. They're treated for any disease they have and neutered so they won't produce kittens. If they're too wild to be tamed, we let them go again in a place where there are no predators or traffic.

"We also have volunteers who take cats, including adult cats, into their homes for socialization. Once the cats are used to being handled, we put them up for adoption. All of the cats you found will be either placed in homes or released in a safe place."

"That's great," Megan said.

Mrs. Colby continued. "We'll pick up those kittens first thing tomorrow morning. Feral kittens are often sick. They may need antibiotics and supplemental feedings with an eyedropper. They may need heat lamps or hot pads to keep them warm. Some feral kittens even need subcutaneous feedings."

"I'll take care of Dinkle," Kylie said. "I'll keep him warm."

"The kittens need to stay with the mother cat for now," Mrs. Colby said.

Instead of going to work Friday afternoon, Lacey Wilcox drove to the police station.

She went to the nearest desk and said, "I have information about that hit-and-run accident where the woman died."

An officer led her into a private office.

"I was driving the other car," Lacey said. Tears trickled down her cheeks as she explained what had happened with the spilled soda. "I panicked," she said. "I've never been so scared."

The officer looked stern. "You should not have left the scene," he said.

"I know. That's why I'm here. I'm sorry about the accident, and I'm sorry I ran away." No matter what happened now, Lacey thought, she had finally done the right thing. "I didn't think we had collided hard enough to injure anyone," she said.

"The crash didn't kill the other driver," the officer said.

"The newspaper said she died."

"The autopsy showed that Mrs. Leefton died of a heart attack. A man mowing his lawn noticed her driving erratically about a block before the intersection. He watched and saw her run the stop sign. He said she never used the brakes, even after you honked at her. The death was not your fault, and the accident was not your fault, either."

Lacey realized that if she had not admitted her part in the accident, she would never have known about the heart attack. She would always have carried the guilt of thinking she had caused a death.

"I'll have to ticket you for leaving the

scene of an accident," the officer said, "but since you turned yourself in, the fine will be reduced."

All Lacey could say was, "I won't lose my job. I can still go to college."

Early the next morning, Officer Rupp arrived to drive Megan to Desolation Hill. "You don't lead a dull life, do you?" he said, when Megan opened the door.

She gave him the note that had been left in the field. "I thought the note was from the driver of the tan car. It turned out to be from Shane Turner."

"You should have called me immediately," Officer Rupp said. "People who write threatening notes are dangerous."

"I found that out," Megan said.

She also gave him the clipping about Lacey Wilcox. "I think she was driving the tan car," Megan said.

"You're right. I've already talked to her."

Officer Rupp drove past the airport. Megan saw two balloons from the festival rise into the air. Watching them, she shuddered with remembered fear.

When they turned off the road onto the path up Desolation Hill, Megan watched carefully for the place where she and Shane had pushed through the underbrush.

She missed it on the way uphill, and they got all the way to the charred remains of the balloon. As they drove back down, Megan spotted the broken branches and trampled weeds. "There!" she cried. "I think that's where we were."

With Officer Rupp following, she found the big fir tree that she had hidden behind. Reenacting the drama of the night before, she crouched down, and dug her fingers in the dirt.

Seconds later, Megan stood and held out the envelope full of money.

"Brice Colby will be happy to see this," Officer Rupp said. "He examined his company's books last night and learned that someone wrote an unauthorized check for over fifteen thousand dollars this week, plus a seven-hundred-dollar check two weeks ago. Both checks were made out to the owner of a nonexistent cement company."

"Can you prove it was Shane?" Megan asked.

"The bank where he cashed the checks had a surveillance camera. The whole transaction is on film."

After Officer Rupp took her home, Megan got out her bag of cat food. She was anxious to go to the field. Even though Mr. Colby had told the bulldozer driver not to continue clearing, Megan was nervous. She wanted to see for herself that the cats were safe.

"Can I go with you?" Kylie asked. "I want to see Dinkle."

Megan started to say no, then remembered Kylie's remark that being lonesome wasn't any fun.

"You can come," Megan said, "but you'll have to be quiet so you don't scare the cats."

Kylie looked surprised. "I'm always quiet," she said.

When the girls arrived at the field, Mrs. Colby and three other volunteers, all wearing thick elbow-length gloves, were there. The bulldozer was gone.

Claws and Pumpkin were in cat carriers, waiting to go to foster homes. Claws meowed and scratched at the carrier door; Pumpkin sat calmly, staring out.

"We think all of these cats will be adoptable," Mrs. Colby said. "We caught those two without using the humane traps. It probably helped that you've been feeding them."

Megan smiled.

"We caught your mother cat and her litter, too. They were in the drainpipe, just as you said. The kittens are small and hungry, but they don't appear to be sick."

"Where are they?" Kylie asked. "I want to see them."

Mrs. Colby pointed to a green van. "They're going home with me," she said. "I'll care for them until they're old enough to be adopted."

Mommacat and her kittens nestled into a soft blanket in a portable dog kennel in the back of Mrs. Colby's van.

Kylie pressed her nose against the van window and looked at the kittens. "There he is!" she said, pointing to a small striped kitten. "There's Dinkle!"

"Our mom said we can adopt two of the kittens when they're ready," Megan explained to Mrs. Colby. "Kylie has already named hers."

"Come and visit the kittens as often as you want," Mrs. Colby said, "so they'll get used to you."

Megan gave Mrs. Colby the bag of cat food, for Mommacat. When it was time to take Dinkle and his sibling home, she would buy kitten food.

One of the other volunteers called, "I have another one!"

Megan recognized Twitchy Tail in the woman's arms.

Kylie began to sing:

"Pet, pet, pet the cat.
Rub him on his fur.
Give him food and keep him warm,
Listen to him purr."

Megan laughed. Her sister's song did not annoy her today.

As she watched the volunteers from Feline Friends, her worries floated away, light as a hot-air balloon. The cats were going to be safe and healthy and loved. All of them.